"If You're Afrai[d] [of Hurting My] Feelings, Don't [Worry, Though.] I Can Take It."

"Okay," he said slowly. "Here goes." He cleared his throat. "Having you here is driving me crazy. I keep thinking about you no matter how hard I try to get you out of my mind. I don't want to be attracted to you. I'm going to marry Cindy."

Janeen stared at him in disbelief. He couldn't be serious! She tried to think of something to say.

He muttered something under his breath and moved toward her. He pulled her to him and kissed her like a man would drink if he was dying of thirst and had just found a gushing fountain. When he finally loosened his hold and stepped back from her, she was almost too weak to stand.

Dear Reader,

There's just something about the mystique of cowboys that continues to fascinate me. THE CRENSHAWS OF TEXAS is the second series I've written about a prominent (and fictional) family from the Lone Star State. What can I say? Characters keep popping into my head demanding their own story.

Man from Stallion Country is the fourth story I've written about the Crenshaws. Jordan Crenshaw, introduced in the first Crenshaw story, *Branded,* meets Janeen White, who first appeared in the second Crenshaw story, *Caught in the Crossfire.* Neither their first meeting nor the idea of a possible relationship goes well for these two.

I enjoyed getting in touch with the Texas clan and hope you will, too. I hope you continue to enjoy all the wonderful Harlequin books during this very special 60th anniversary year. Happy birthday, Harlequin!

Sincerely,

Annette Broadrick

ANNETTE BROADRICK

MAN FROM STALLION COUNTRY

Silhouette® Desire

Published by Silhouette Books

America's Publisher of Contemporary Romance

SILHOUETTE BOOKS

Recycling programs
for this product may
not exist in your area.

ISBN-13: 978-0-373-76918-6
ISBN-10:   0-373-76918-0

MAN FROM STALLION COUNTRY

Copyright © 2009 by Annette Broadick

Visit Silhouette Books at www.eHarlequin.com

Printed in U.S.A.

ANNETTE BROADRICK

believes in romance and the magic of life. Since 1984, Annette has shared her view of life and love with readers. In addition to being nominated by *Romantic Times BOOKreviews* magazine as one of the Best New Authors of that year, she has also won the Reviewers' Choice Award for Best in Series; the *Romantic Times BOOKreviews* WISH award and Lifetime Achievement Awards for Series Romance and Series Romantic Fantasy.

To the men and women who are overseas to protect us. Words cannot begin to express how proud we are of you for the tough job you're doing. We love you and continue to pray for your safety and homecoming.

One

Janeen White's first trip to Texas to visit her good friend Lindsey Crenshaw really opened her eyes to Southwestern hospitality. She took in the scene around her with amazement and acknowledged that the Crenshaws certainly knew how to throw a party.

The sprawling live oak trees scattered across the vast lawn were covered in fairy lights. Musicians played country music near a large patio where people were dancing. The delicious aroma of barbecue wafted through the air, and several tables holding vast quantities of food teased the senses. Long picnic tables sat among the trees and people stood in line to fill their plates.

The clear sky with a full moon put the finishing touch on the festivities.

Janeen and Lindsey sat in lawn chairs out of the traffic area and watched the dancers, the various groups of men and women talking and laughing and others filling their plates with food.

The two women had been friends for years, ever since they'd first met while attending Georgetown University in Washington, D.C. Janeen loved Georgetown, but to get there, she had had to defy her mother, who wanted her to go to school in New England. She'd had to deal with weekly calls from said mother, telling her about every crime that had been reported anywhere near Washington. Lindsey had listened sympathetically to Janeen's laments about her mother, who felt it her right and duty to organize Janeen's life.

Since Lindsey had grown up without a mother, she'd found the stories fascinating, even funny at times. The bond created between the two had lasted for years.

After graduation, Janeen had taken a job at the Metropolitan Museum of Art, in Manhattan, and Lindsay had married Jared Crenshaw and moved to Texas. But they had always kept in touch. In fact, a few years ago Lindsey had lived with Janeen in her New York apartment during a particularly bad patch in Lindsey and Jared's marriage.

She would never forget the day she opened the door to her apartment to find standing before her a tall, well-built hunk with gorgeous blue eyes dressed in cowboy garb, asking for Lindsey. She could immediately see why Lindsey was so crazy about him.

When Lindsey had returned to Houston with her husband, the two friends continued to stay in touch by e-mail and long phone conversations. Lindsey extended an open invitation for Janeen to come down and visit her, and Janeen had assured Lindsey that one of these days she'd take her up on her offer.

When the Met had had to cut back and Janeen suddenly found herself without a job, she'd called Lindsey for consolation. Instead of commiserating with her, Lindsey had pressed her to come down to Texas to visit for an extended stay and forget her life in New York for a while.

The offer couldn't have come at a better time. Steve was becoming a problem. She'd been casually dating him until she found out that he was nothing like he'd first appeared to be. Then she'd stopped going out with him. He didn't want to take no for an answer and kept phoning and dropping by to see her at work and her apartment.

If she left town for a while, he would hopefully forget about her and move on. Visiting Texas had sounded like just the answer for her.

She'd been in Texas for a week now. She'd had a chance to say hello and goodbye to Jared before he took off on another one of his extended trips overseas. Once he left, she and Lindsey stayed busy catching up on everything that hadn't been discussed by phone and e-mail. Janeen also took the opportunity to get to know Lindsey and Jared's three children after years of seeing them only in photographs.

For some time the children had been pleading to go visit their cousins in Central Texas. By the end of the week, Lindsey decided to go in order to escape the heat and high humidity of Houston—located on the Texas coast—and to give Janeen the opportunity to see more of the state.

Once they had arrived at the ranch, Janeen could better understand why the children begged to come here. Jared's older brother, Jake, his wife, Ashley, and their children lived in the hacienda-style Crenshaw family home.

The home was big enough to get lost in—more like a hotel—and truly historic. Crenshaws had lived there for generations. There were so many outbuildings that when the two women had arrived yesterday afternoon, Janeen thought at first the place was a village.

When Jake and Ashley decided to have a barbecue in her honor, Janeen had been taken aback until Lindsey had laughingly explained that the Crenshaws used any excuse to throw a barbecue and invite everyone around.

Janeen could definitely believe it. She'd met so many Crenshaws since she'd arrived that her head was spinning. Grandfathers and fathers and uncles and aunts and so many cousins she'd lost count. All of them were welcoming and friendly.

She was in another world, nothing like the one she was

from. The men were certainly eye-catching. Janeen wished she'd brought a camera to prove to friends in New York that such men really existed—tall, tanned, broad-shouldered, self-confident and brimming with sex appeal.

Even though she wasn't looking for a relationship with anyone these days, she could certainly enjoy the view.

"You're awfully quiet," Lindsey said, interrupting the comfortable silence between old friends.

Janeen looked at her and smiled. "This is all so amazing. I had no idea such a place existed."

"Oh, you mean the hacienda? The first Crenshaw bought this land in the early 1840s before Texas became a state. The descendants take pride in ensuring that their legacy will be passed down for years to come."

Janeen looked over at the huge smoker where Jake tended the meat—beef, chicken and pork ribs—and inhaled the delicious aroma. "Everyone seems to know everyone else," she said.

"Do you remember that I met Jared at one of these gatherings?"

Janeen smiled. "Couldn't have it more romantic than this, I must admit. Who needs New York when you can have this kind of entertainment for free?"

She noticed a big shiny black four-door pickup truck drive up and park by the barn. She idly watched the driver step down out of the truck and thread his way through the many cars and trucks in the driveway.

"Don't tell me. Let me guess," she said with a grin, nodding toward the newcomer. "The newest arrival has to be a Crenshaw."

Lindsey followed Janeen's glance. "You're right. That's Jordan Crenshaw, Jared and Jake's cousin."

Janeen watched as Jordan sauntered across the lawn, pausing to speak to some of the guests and waving to others while slowly heading toward Jake.

"Hmm," Lindsey said, "I wonder where his fiancée is? According to Ashley, everyone in the family was caught by surprise when Jordan casually mentioned to Jake that he and

Cindy O'Neil were engaged. Her dad owns a ranch somewhere around here."

"Jordan's a rancher, too?"

"He raises and breeds quarter horses. Jared once commented that he was convinced Jordan preferred the company of his horses to most human beings."

Janeen glanced over at him again. "Is he some kind of recluse?"

"According to Jared he's shy, first of all. Add to that the fact that he was badly hurt by a woman. He dated somebody at Texas A&M the last semester of their senior year. After graduation she moved back home, somewhere near D.C., I think."

"What happened?"

"Although he didn't see her after she moved back East, they talked on the phone. I guess being apart made Jordan realize how much he missed her and loved her. Her family had horses, which was another reason Jordan thought they could have a life together. He gathered up his nerve to go see her with a ring in his pocket. Knowing Jordan, he wouldn't have gone if he wasn't fairly sure she'd say yes."

"Don't stop now. What happened?"

Lindsey shrugged. "I guess she didn't feel the same way about him. Once back home, she'd started dating someone else. He was really torn up over the whole thing. He withdrew from everyone and devoted himself to his horses.

"So you can see why I was surprised to hear about the engagement. It's a good sign, though. Must mean that he's gotten over his college sweetheart. Jared told me to find out when they planned to marry because he would put it on his schedule at work. The Crenshaws are big on family, as you can tell. So of course we'll make sure to be here for their wedding."

"I take it he's an only child."

"Oh, no. He has a twin brother, Jack, but Jack isn't interested in ranching. He travels around the country, following the rodeo circuit. He's won all kinds of prizes."

Janeen smiled. "Good for him."

Lindsey grinned. In a teasing voice she said, "I was disappointed to hear about Jordan's engagement. I'd planned to introduce the two of you."

Janeen frowned. "Why?"

"I thought he might get your mind off that idiot you were dating—Steve."

"I was not in love with Steve," she replied. "I thought it was a little odd that he kept suggesting I introduce him to my parents. I finally took him to Connecticut—one time, mind you—and then I realized he just wanted an in with Dad's corporation. I was disappointed because I was fond of him, and I thought he cared about me. What he really cared about was advancing his career. So at the moment, I'm not particularly interested in meeting somebody new."

"You never told Steve why you called it quits, right?"

"No."

"And so he started calling and dropping in on you."

Janeen smiled. "He hated to see his career opportunity slipping away."

Both of them laughed.

"Maybe he really was in love with you."

"Not a chance. At least he won't bother me here in Texas. Hopefully by the time I go back, he will have accepted defeat."

They sat quietly and continued watching people until Lindsey said, "I don't know about you, but I can't resist the smell of that barbecue any longer. Let's go get some, okay?"

Janeen laughed. "Thank goodness. I've been drooling just from the aroma."

When they reached the food line, Lindsey introduced Janeen to several of the people around them. Once again, Janeen was amazed by everyone's friendliness. She was really touched.

While standing in line, Janeen glanced around at the tables. Most of them looked full. Maybe they should have come to eat sooner.

She and Lindsey filled their plates from the various dishes

set out on one long table. There was German potato salad, coleslaw, baked beans and Texas toast—and that was before they reached the barbecued meat. Janeen felt embarrassed for piling her plate so high until she saw that not only Lindsey but everyone else held similar plates.

Once through the line, Lindsey paused beside her. "Looks like we waited too long. All the tables are full. Oh, wait. There's one over there," she said and headed to one of the tables that wasn't easily visible. Two men sat at the table nestled in the shadows of one of the large trees. "Let's go before anyone else gets there."

As they approached, Janeen recognized one of the men as the Crenshaw cousin. What was his name?

Lindsey asked, "Mind if we join you?"

One of them spoke. "Not at all," and Janeen realized it was the other man who had replied.

Once seated, Lindsey said, "Janeen, I'd like you to meet Tom Grayson. He's a banker. And this is Jordan Crenshaw. Jordan has a horse ranch not far from here. Gentlemen, this is my very good friend, Janeen White."

Janeen nodded to both men, smiled and said, "Hello."

Jordan paused from eating and looked at her without smiling. "Hello," he replied and continued to eat. Tom grinned, looking at her with undisguised interest and said, "Pleased to meet you, ma'am. Janeen, you say?"

"That's right."

"Well, if you're looking for some fine fixings, you've come to the right place. These Crenshaws really know how to put on a spread, that's for sure." When he finally stopped looking at Janeen, he turned to Lindsey and asked, "Where's Jared? I haven't seen him." He glanced around with a slight frown.

"Oh, he didn't come with us, Tom. He's traveling on business and won't be back for a few weeks," Lindsey replied.

There wasn't much more conversation during the meal. It was only after the plates were almost empty that Lindsey said, "Jordan, I understand congratulations are in order."

He straightened and looked at her, reaching for his longneck bottle of beer. He took a drink before he answered. "Thanks," he said. He picked up a rib and began to eat it.

Not to be put off when she was looking for information, Lindsey asked, "Where is Cindy tonight?"

Jordan wiped his hands on one of the large paper towels and said, "She couldn't come. She said it looked as if her dad was coming down with the flu, and she didn't want to leave him, so I came on over here by myself."

Lindsey smiled. "I'm glad you came. I haven't seen you in more than a year."

Jordan looked around at the other people. "Are your children here?"

Lindsey replied, "Oh, yes. They're in that group chasing each other around the trees. They've been begging to come spend some time over here. They definitely have the Crenshaw blood in them. They would much prefer to live in the country than in Houston. I have to admit there's a great deal to do here."

They all continued to eat until Tom looked at Janeen and said, "So you're here visiting, I take it?"

Janeen nodded, her mouth full. Lindsey came to her rescue. "Yes, she is. I can't tell you how much I'm enjoying her being here. I've been trying to get her to come to Texas for years. Janeen recently took a leave of absence from the museum in Manhattan where she works and decided to come spend some time with us."

Janeen swallowed, took a quick drink from her glass of iced tea and shook her head. "No point in pretending, Lindsey." She looked at the men. "I was fired."

"Laid off," Lindsey said.

Janeen sighed. "Whatever you call it, I'm unemployed." She looked at Jordan. "I understand you raise horses. My dad has a stable, and he's kept horses as far back as I can remember. I spent more time in the stable than I did in the house when I was growing up. Do you have an opening, by any chance? I can muck out stalls with the best of them."

Lindsey and Tom burst out laughing. "This is supposed to be a vacation, sweetie," Lindsey said. "You'll have plenty of time to look for work once you go back home."

Jordan finished his meal, carefully cleaned his hands, finished off his beer and only then did he look at Janeen. This woman, dressed in obviously expensive clothes, with her carefully coifed light blond hair and exquisite makeup, was obviously making a joke at his expense. His imagination wasn't vivid enough to imagine a woman like her mucking out stalls.

"What sort of work are you looking for?" Jordan drawled, irritated by the silly games some women played.

"I don't care," she replied. "Exercise them?" she suggested. "Clean stalls? Whatever needs to be done."

"Somehow, I don't think those flimsy high-heeled sandals you're wearing would be of much practical use at my place."

She eyed him uncertainly. "Well, of course I have other shoes. Lindsey told me I'd probably be riding while I'm here."

Jordan shook his head. She almost sounded sincere. Too bad. Jake had horses for her to ride here. Jordan was certain she could find a stall or two to clean without leaving the place.

"I think I'll pass, but thanks for the offer," he said, knowing he sounded sarcastic but he didn't care. Let her find someone else to play her little games with. He stood, picking up his plate and bottle. "Have a good visit," he added before he looked at Tom. "Tom, I'll give you a call tomorrow about the auction." He smiled at Lindsey. "Good to see you again, Lindsey. Be sure to tell Jared hello for me."

"Will do," she said.

Janeen waited until Tom had taken Jordan's lead and left them sitting by themselves before she asked, "Did I imagine it, or did I detect a hint of sarcasm from Mr. Crenshaw?"

"He was teasing you. He knew you had no intention of going to work for him."

Janeen flushed. "Why? It's not like I don't have experience working around horses," she replied.

"Have you looked in the mirror lately?" Lindsey asked, grinning from ear to ear. "You look much too fragile to clean out stalls and perform other heavy work."

Feeling disgruntled, Janeen muttered, "He couldn't even see my shoes." She didn't like the way she felt at his total rejection of her. She didn't need some hotshot cowboy giving her a bad time.

"Oh, he saw them," Lindsey replied, obviously fighting not to smile. "Didn't you see him looking you over when we were walking to his table? I'm sure he didn't miss a thing about you."

Janeen looked over at the barbecue pit and saw Jordan talking to Jake. "I'm surprised he found someone willing to marry him, with his attitude." She looked back at Lindsey and shrugged. "I'll admit I wasn't too impressed with the guy, but so what? It isn't as though I'll ever see him again, right?"

Two

Five days after the barbecue, Jordan's cell phone rang as he walked to his house from the barn. The sun was barely peeking over the horizon. He'd spent most of the night in the foaling barn and wanted nothing more at the moment than a long, hot shower, some breakfast and a chance to get some sleep.

A ringing phone didn't bode well for his plans. It was either a client wanting to bring a prized mare over to be serviced or someone who had heard about his horse ranch and wanted to board and/or have an animal broken to ride. Couldn't they have put off the call until later in the day?

He dug his phone out of his shirt pocket with a sigh.

"Crenshaw," he said tersely.

"Hey, Jordan. It's Jake. I hope I didn't wake you up."

"That will be the day. As a matter of fact, I haven't been to bed yet. Spent the night in the barn with one of my mares. How's it going?"

Jake sighed. "Not so well."

Jordan frowned. He and Jake had been closer than brothers for years. It was Jake who had encouraged Jordan to follow his dream to work with horses rather than raise cattle or sheep. Anytime things weren't going well for Jake, Jordan would do whatever he could for him.

"What's wrong?"

"Joey woke up this morning running a high fever and covered in chicken pox."

"Oh, man. Just what you needed, right?"

"The doctor has quarantined all five children since Lindsey's kids have been exposed."

"You really are going to have your hands full. I figured Lindsey would be back in Houston by now."

"Nope. They're still here."

"Well, you know if there's anything I can do for you, just name it." Jordan figured he could take up some of the slack with ranch chores and give Jake more time to stay close to the house.

Jake sighed. "Better wait until you hear the favor I'm asking before you start volunteering."

"Doesn't matter. You helped me get my business going there at your place until I could afford to build what I needed here, and you wouldn't take a nickel for it. I figure I definitely owe you."

"You don't owe me anything, and you know it. However, if you'll do this one little thing for me, I'll be forever in your debt."

"No problem. Who do I have to kill, and where do you want me to hide the body?"

Jake laughed. "It's not that bad. Ashley and Lindsey are going to be busy with the kids for the next few days."

"That must be tough, since staying inside when they can be out riding will not appeal to the children. Do you need me to come over and help out? I can do that, you know. Whatever you need."

Instead of responding to his offer, Jake changed the subject.

"Did you meet Lindsey's friend the other night when you were here for the barbecue?"

"Yeah, why?"

"Well, Lindsey's upset that Janeen's going to be stuck here at the house with irritable kids. I understand that Janeen has offered to go back to New York early, but Lindsey doesn't want her to leave."

Jordan decided he must be more tired than he realized. He was having trouble following the conversation. He'd reached the house by this time and wearily let himself in the back door, his hunting hound, Gus, following him inside.

"What does that have to do with asking me for a favor?"

"As it so happens, it's the very reason I'm calling."

Jordan removed his hat and hung it on the wall. He sat in one of the kitchen chairs, feeling exhaustion taking over. He ran his hand through his hair. "Sorry, Jake. I'm having trouble following you. Why don't you give me time to get some sleep, and I'll come over there this afternoon, okay?"

"You can help me by staying right there and letting Janeen stay with you for the next few days."

Jordan shook his head. He couldn't have heard what he thought Jake said. When Jake didn't say anything else, Jordan carefully repeated what he thought he'd just heard.

"You want her to stay here with me?" Jordan asked in disbelief.

"That's right."

Before he could stop them, words tumbled out of his mouth. "Are you out of your cotton-picking mind? I've never had any woman stay here with me. Not even Cindy. Can't you find someplace else?"

"Probably, but bear with me for a minute. At the moment you're the closest family I have to call on, geographically, at least. Jason and Leslie left two days ago on vacation. Jude's the only other brother I can ask and, as you know, he lives in Maryland. So now I'm looking to my cousins. Since you've already met her, I figured you'd be the one to call."

No. Absolutely not. He didn't want that woman anywhere

around him. He shouldn't have agreed before finding out what Jake wanted from him.

Jordan cleared his throat. "Here's the problem, Jake. I'm not really good at entertaining people, especially women, and this house is definitely a bachelor's place. It's small and far from fancy. I doubt very much that she'd want to stay here, of all places. She probably thinks everyone in the family lives in a sprawling home like yours."

Jake didn't say anything. The silence stretched between them for too long before Jake finally said, "I take it you don't like her."

Jordan almost groaned out loud. "I didn't say that."

"You didn't have to, Jordan. I can tell."

Jordan wished they could have this conversation once he'd caught up on his sleep. "I don't dislike her, exactly. I just know the type, that's all. She'll be bored within hours, I guarantee you, and wanting to go sightseeing or something. I don't have time to do that at the moment." Or at anytime in the next twenty years or so. Possibly thirty years.

"Come on, Jordan. Just because she's classy and beautiful and blond doesn't mean she's anything like Stephanie. And even if she is, so what? I would just like to find her a place to stay where she can relax and not listen to kids whining for a few days. I'm not asking you to marry the woman, for pete's sake."

"Good to know. I already have one fiancée. But here's another thing. There's just something about her that makes me uncomfortable."

She'd popped into his mind a few times since the night he'd met her, which really ticked him off. He'd always been susceptible to fragile-looking blondes, which is how he got in trouble by falling for Stephanie. She'd never said she thought she was better than he was, but her rejection made him feel that she did. At least he hadn't made a complete fool of himself by actually proposing to her.

He was definitely over Steph. He just didn't need someone like her underfoot to remind him of that particular weakness of his.

"Could the fact that she's centerfold material be bothering you?"

Jordan sighed. "You noticed," he drawled. "I don't know what to say to someone like her."

"Maybe Cindy can help out."

"She's staying pretty close to home these days. Her dad isn't bouncing back from the flu like they expected. She's trying to get him to go into town to see Dr. Lawson. She's not having much luck at the moment, though. So she's keeping a close watch on him."

"Okay," Jake said, sounding tired. "Bottom line. Will you or won't you let Janeen come stay with you?"

Jordan dropped his head and rubbed the back of his neck. He might as well give in and make the best of what was going to be an extremely awkward situation. "Do you want me to come get her?"

"No. Why don't you get some rest? I'll have Lindsey bring her over sometime this afternoon, if that's all right with you."

"Guess it'll have to be." He knew he sounded less than gracious.

"Thank you, Jordan. I want you to know that I truly appreciate you doing this for me."

"Okay. Oh, and, Jake?"

"Yeah?"

"Just so you know. You're definitely going to owe me for this. Big-time!"

Jake hung up laughing.

Jordan looked at his watch. Before he could get some sleep he'd need to clear out the extra bedroom. He used it mostly for storage, but there was a bed in there somewhere. Of course it might take a bulldozer to find it.

He started a pot of coffee before he got in the shower. The sooner he got started the quicker he'd be able to go to bed.

"This is a really bad idea, Lindsey," Janeen said later that afternoon. "I really think I should fly back to New York and come back to visit you a little later."

While she talked, Janeen took in the scenery of the Hill Country. The road wound through the countryside like a ribbon.

"I know you didn't care for Jordan when you first met him, but he's agreed to have you stay, just until we know if we can take the children home. Please indulge me in this, okay?" Lindsey gave her a quick glance. "If my kids don't come down with chicken pox—and they may not, you know—you'll only be there a few days. After that we'll have several weeks to explore the state before you need to go back. I've been counting on this visit so much. Jared said he felt a little better about leaving me this time knowing that you would be here for company."

"Make me feel guilty, why don't you? But why Jordan, of all people? I could get a room at one of the motels in town, you know."

"And do what? Stare at the walls? You wanted to see Jordan's horses, didn't you? Well, now's your chance."

Janeen looked at her with exasperation. "Visiting for a couple of hours is a far cry from moving in with the guy! Won't his fiancée be upset?"

Lindsey shrugged. "She may already live there, you know. I'm sure she'll be willing to show you around the area, maybe go horseback riding, that sort of thing. You probably won't have to spend much time with Jordan, anyway. I know I'm asking a lot from you, but I'm pleading here. Do this for me, okay?"

Great. She either spent a day or two with a man she hadn't expected to see again—and, by the way, had been pleased with the prospect—or hurt Lindsey's feelings. Not that any of this mattered, since she'd caved and agreed to go earlier in the day. She'd just thought she would try once again.

"Did you say that Jordan's place was close by Jake's? We've been on the road for almost an hour."

"It isn't all that far as the bird flies. There just isn't a direct route from one place to the other. They're no more than sixty or seventy miles apart."

"Practically neighbors, wouldn't you say?"

Lindsey laughed. "When we measure distance in Texas, we

go by the hours it takes to get somewhere, not the miles. There's his gate just ahead. See, that wasn't so bad."

"Where's his house?"

"Just a few more miles. We'll see it soon."

Janeen groaned. "This is unbelievable."

Once they passed the rock entrance, they followed a lane that wandered through meadows, over hills and down through dry creek beds.

"What do you do if it rains? Don't the creek beds fill up?"

"You bet. You wait until they go down, which they do. Eventually."

"Swell."

She had to admit that the ranch was truly beautiful, with its white fences, scattered live oak trees and grazing pastures. Maybe she was making too big a deal about staying here. After all, she loved horses. She would enjoy riding through some of the hills, communing with nature. She'd steer clear of her host, who was no doubt as reluctant to have her here as she was about staying here, no matter what Jake had told them.

Well, she'd probably be here for only a day or two.

Jordan watched from the porch as Lindsey turned in front of his house in her SUV. With the tinted windows, he couldn't see who was inside but he already knew. Janeen White had arrived for her visit.

His hound, Gus, stuck his head beneath Jordan's fingers, looking for some head scratching. Jordan absently stroked Gus's head before he took a deep breath and exhaled when the women got out of the car. Despite the casualness of her jeans and cotton shirt, Janeen looked like she'd just stepped off a fashion show runway. She had "family money" written all over her. Probably a former debutante slumming for a few days.

She wore her hair down this morning, and it glowed like spun silver and gold. She'd worn it pulled back from her face into some kind of fancy knot at the barbecue. The length of her hair surprised him for some reason. It tumbled around her shoulders. He doubted that blond was her natural hair color.

She looked artificial from the top of her shiny head to the painted toes that showed in the sandals she wore.

Jordan and Gus stepped off the porch and met them near the SUV. "Good afternoon, ladies." He slipped his fingers around Gus's collar. Maybe she didn't like dogs...or was allergic to them. Wouldn't that be a shame?

Lindsey answered, "Jake mentioned that you were up most of the night. I hope you managed to get some sleep today."

"Enough, thanks."

"I really appreciate your willingness to have company for a few days."

He glanced at Janeen and discovered she had the darkest blue eyes he'd ever seen. He'd thought they were brown the other night. She'd taken off her sunglasses when she stepped out of the car, and now that he was looking at her, she nervously put them back on. Maybe she was feeling as awkward as he was about this situation.

Jordan cleared his throat. "I guess we need to get your luggage out of the car." He started toward the back of the SUV, and Janeen followed him.

"I can get them," Janeen said quickly. "You don't need to—" She stopped speaking when he ignored her, reached in and picked up two suitcases that matched and walked toward the house without a word.

Janeen watched him walk away before she turned to Lindsey and said, "Oh, this is going to be fun. Jordan acts as though I'm going to be doing a root canal on him. Can't you tell? He's definitely not happy about the arrangements."

"You're imagining things. Jake said Jordan was okay with it. I think you're reading something into his behavior that just isn't there."

"He certainly isn't in a very good mood."

"He's probably still tired from being up all night...and don't forget that he's shy. He never has much to say to anybody, not just you. Once he gets to know you a little better, I'm sure he'll relax more."

"I can only hope," Janeen muttered under her breath.

Lindsey heard her and laughed. "Would you stop worrying? Everything's going to work out just fine. If you decide you really don't want to stay, all you need to do is call me, and I'll come get you. Plus, I'll keep in close touch with you. In the meantime, have fun."

Lindsey got back into the car and left. Janeen did her best not to feel abandoned in enemy territory.

She might as well go inside. With a great deal of reluctance, Janeen followed the flagstone walkway that Jordan had taken and went into the house. She stepped into a large kitchen and was greeted by Gus.

Janeen said, "Hello, there, fella. Aren't you a good-looking guy." Gus responded by wagging his tail. She let him sniff her hand for a moment before she straightened and looked around.

The kitchen had plenty of cabinets and counter space, up-to-date appliances and a small round table with chairs arranged around it in one of the corners. The kitchen looked warm and welcoming.

She stood there, unsure of where she should go. After a couple of minutes, Jordan stuck his head around the open doorway that led to the rest of the house. "There you are." He sounded irritated. "Let me show you where you'll be sleeping."

If he hadn't wanted her here, why hadn't he just said so when Jake called him? He didn't have to be so abrupt.

She followed him down the hallway and paused in the doorway of what she presumed to be the bedroom she would be using. He stepped back, and she went into the room.

Her suitcases were near the door, waiting for her. There were some boxes stacked in one corner of the room. A dresser with a mirror, a bed and an end table with a lamp completed the furniture in the room. There was nothing on the walls.

She turned to Jordan. "Thank you," she said politely. "This looks very comfortable."

"Your bathroom is across the hall," he nodded his head in that direction. "I have one off my bedroom so you'll have it to yourself."

"All right." She paused, searching for words. "Does your fiancée live here?"

He frowned. "Of course not. Is that what you're used to back East? Living together before you get married?"

She counted to ten. Then she repeated the count. Finally, she was able to say with a calmness she didn't feel, "Not necessarily, no. I wondered how she felt about me staying here."

"I haven't told her yet. I'm sure she won't have a problem with it." He turned on his heel. "I'll see you later," he said over his shoulder.

She heard the kitchen door open and close before she realized that she'd been holding her breath. Whew. The man had to have flunked charm school.

Janeen took her time unpacking. She'd brought several styles of dress from New York, uncertain what she'd be doing while she was here. From the looks of things, she would spend most of her time in jeans, which was okay with her.

After she finished unpacking, Janeen wandered through the house. She'd seen several homes built this way since she'd been in the state. The plan was ranch-style, according to Lindsey. There was a large living room that held a couple of recliner chairs with a table between them, a stone fireplace and the latest in televisions. He obviously didn't do much entertaining. However, there were framed pictures on the wall, and she took her time looking at each one.

A dated wedding picture of a smiling couple who were probably his parents was next to several others. There was one of the same couple holding a pair of infants. Others showed Jordan and his brother as they grew older. They really looked alike, the older they got. How did anyone tell them apart?

There were no pictures of his fiancée. He probably kept them in his room.

Another room was obviously being used as an office. A large desk was covered in papers and files. She wondered if he'd like to have her file for him.

Probably not.

As she continued to explore, Janeen noted that each room in the house had at least one large window that framed the rolling hills and large trees surrounding the house.

The only magazines she'd seen lying around were about horses. Not that it mattered. She was too keyed up to be able to sit down and read, anyway. She decided to go outside and explore.

Janeen almost laughed out loud when she walked into the horse barn and looked around. The barn was much more luxurious than the house. She saw a couple of men cleaning out stalls.

"Hello," she said to the men.

They glanced up and did a double take. "Hello," one of them said. "May I help you?"

"No, thank you. I hope it's all right for me to look around." They glanced at each other. "I'm staying here for the next few days," she added, which caused another shared look.

"If you're looking for Jordan, he was just here. I can call him—"

"Oh, no, that's all right."

She left, recognizing their uneasiness. She probably should have waited for Jordan to show her around.

The horses in the pasture looked strong and healthy. Their coats were like satin, and she itched to ride one. She would definitely have to wait until Jordan okayed that idea. Plus, she would need to get used to a western saddle, which shouldn't be too difficult.

While in the barn, Janeen had picked up an escort—a mixed-breed dog that was part spaniel. She had come bouncing out of one of the stalls and seemed excited to see her, giving her the warmest greeting she'd received since she'd arrived.

Janeen wandered around for about a half hour before she decided to go back to the house, accompanied by her new friend. The dog was cute with black and white splotches all over her, as though she'd been playing in paint. She looked young and lonesome.

At least Janeen had some company. As soon as she sat in one of the rocking chairs on the porch, the dog settled at her feet. The roofline shaded the porch, and there was a slight breeze. She heard a soft noise and looked at her feet. Her companion was gently snoring.

The walk had relaxed Janeen somewhat, and she leaned back into the chair, allowing the gentle motion to soothe her. She closed her eyes and listened to the birds singing as a gentle breeze rustled in the trees around the house.

She drifted into a half awake, half asleep state.

Jordan found Janeen asleep when he and Gus returned to the house. Feisty lifted her head at his approach, her tail thumping against the wooden porch. Gus walked over and checked her out before throwing himself on the floor and closing his eyes.

Something roused Janeen and she opened her eyes to find Jordan leaning against the porch railing. "Oh! Hi."

"I understand you were looking for me earlier," he said brusquely. "What did you need?"

"I really wasn't looking for you. I just thought I'd look around and get a little exercise. I hope that was okay."

"Oh."

When the silence became awkward, Janeen asked, "I was wondering if I could ride one of your horses while I'm here."

His jaw tightened. "Not alone. I'll take you riding when I'm not too busy. If you'll excuse me, I need to go check on a couple of my mares since you weren't looking for me."

He said the last words as he went down the porch steps. He couldn't make it clearer that she was already a nuisance.

Well. Nuisance or not, she wanted to see the horses. With that in mind, she followed him, the two dogs trailing behind them. By the time she reached the stable doors, he was nowhere to be seen.

What a jerk.

Now that he was out there somewhere, she decided to take a closer look at his quarter horses. Most were out in the pastures, including a black stallion that had his own private corral near the barn.

She approached the fence slowly. When the stallion saw her, he took off running around the perimeter of the fence, the whites of his eyes showing. He was scared of her. She wondered why. When he stopped, he was as far away as possible in the small pasture. He whinnied and flicked his mane, not taking his eyes off her.

"My goodness, you're beautiful," she said softly. "A little thin, maybe. I bet I could find some carrots in the house, if you'd like."

He gave his head a shake and took a step back.

"Well, maybe not. Can't we be friends?"

"No, you can't."

Janeen jumped at the sound of a voice directly behind her. Jordan stepped around her and leaned against the wooden fence, watching the stallion.

"He's beautiful."

"Yes, and he can be deadly. I've been working with him, attempting to get him used to people. He's abused. His owner said he'd merely been trying to break him for riding. What the man had done was criminal. A scared horse can be a dangerous one. I don't want you anywhere around him, you understand?"

She turned her gaze from the horse to the man next to her. She snapped to attention and saluted. "Yes, sir, mi capitan!"

He gave her a look that would melt lead at ten paces. "Are you making fun of me, Ms. White?"

"Not at all, Mr. Crenshaw. You may have forgotten that I was brought up around horses. I'm not a novice where they're concerned."

"Never said you were."

She looked around at another pasture that held a half dozen horses. "Are any of those riding horses?"

"All of them are." He adjusted his hat, pulling it low over his brow. "Now, if you'll excuse me." He turned and headed back to the barn.

How had he known she was out here? Did he have an extra set of eyes? Well, of course. The two men working there earlier must have spotted her.

She turned and began to walk along a lane that led to the steeper hills of the ranch, with the dogs following her. She'd gone about a half mile when she heard a sharp whistle. She turned around and there her kind and charismatic host stood with his hands on his hips. When she turned, he motioned for her to come back.

Janeen took her time, tamping down her anger. When she came up to him, she said, "Would you like to get an ankle lock to monitor my movements?" She smiled sweetly.

"Look, you're my responsibility as long as you're here. You have never been in the Hill Country before, and I see no reason for you to put yourself in danger because you're bored."

"I'm not bored. Just curious. As you say, I've never been exploring on a ranch."

"There's a reason for that. Those hills harbor predators."

"Oh? Lions and tigers and bears, perhaps?"

"More like cougars and coyotes and rattlesnakes," he replied drily.

She turned and looked down the lane. After a minute she turned back to him. "I can ride out there, though, right?"

"Never by yourself. Too many things can happen. Your

mount can be startled by quail, rabbits or snakes and throw you before you know what happened."

She cocked her head. "Has that ever happened to you?"

"How do you think I found out what startles a horse? Of course it has."

She sighed. "Okay." What was she going to do? Finally, she asked, "May I borrow a car to drive to town? I'll buy some books and magazines to read and stay out of your hair."

He frowned. "Okay."

"Great!" she replied with fake heartiness. At least he hadn't said no to those plans. She started for the house.

"Have you ever driven a truck?" he called out from behind her.

She continued toward the house. "No, but how hard can it be?" she replied, hurrying to get her purse before he changed his mind.

She ran up the steps to the porch.

She'd adapt. She didn't need to be patronized. Despite his allowing her to stay there, she had no illusions about him wanting her there. He didn't have to be quite so pointed in his irritation. The other Crenshaws she'd met had been friendly and welcoming. She'd gotten stuck with the one who didn't like people.

Lucky her.

Once inside the house, she changed into one of her dresses, combed her hair and checked her makeup. Then she grabbed her purse and walked out of the house. Jordan stood by a large truck, the big, black one she'd seen him in the night of the barbecue.

It was much bigger than she'd first thought. There was a step up for the driver to get into the cab. When Jordan saw her, he moved to the front of the truck. Once she reached his side, he took her arm and propelled her around to the passenger side. "Do you expect me to drive from over here?" she asked.

"No. I don't expect you to drive at all. Get in. I'm taking you to town."

Every time Jordan stood close to her, he could smell the light floral scent she wore. It drove him crazy. He didn't want to be moved by her at all.

He placed his hands on either side of her waist and lifted her into the seat. She'd gasped as soon as he touched her. For good reason. Touching her had created a spark that should have set off spontaneous combustion. As soon as her butt was in the seat, he released her, stepped back and shut the door.

She waited until he got into the truck and then said, "I take it you don't want me driving your truck."

He reversed and swung the truck around before driving to the highway. "You said you'd never driven a truck before, which tells me you wouldn't be used to one this size."

"Oh."

"It's easier to drive you than to teach you how to get around in this thing without running into something. Besides, I have some things I need to pick up in town, anyway."

She was blessedly quiet for the rest of the way. He turned on the radio to discourage any conversation, but all the while he was very aware of her.

Stop thinking about her. You're engaged. Think about Cindy.

Maybe he'd have Cindy over for dinner tonight. No, that wouldn't work. She wouldn't leave her dad. He supposed that he'd have to adjust to the fact that he and Janeen would be eating together for the foreseeable future.

Now there was something to look forward to.

Once they reached town, Jordan drove to the town square and parked.

"Most of the stores are around here," he said. "I've got some things to pick up, so why don't we meet at the café across the street in about a half hour?"

"All right," she said quietly and reached for the door handle.

"Wait. I'll help you down. It takes a little time to get used to the height."

He barely heard her mumble, "No kidding."

He walked around the truck. A horn sounded and he glanced around, waving at a friend. He reached the door and opened it. "You dismount as if you're on a horse—backward. Grab the

hand grip just inside the cab and lower yourself to the step."
He stood close enough to catch her if her foot slipped. Otherwise, he allowed her to get out of the truck on her own.

Once on the ground, she turned and faced him. "Thank you."

He tugged on his hat brim. "You're welcome. I'll see you in a half hour or so."

Once back in the truck, Jordan left the area for the feed store. There was always something to pick up whenever anyone from the ranch came into town.

He spent time visiting with the owner and some of the men sitting around. After making certain the feed had been put in the back of the truck, he took his leave and drove back to the square, parking in front of the café.

When he walked in, he saw a couple of men standing near one of the booths, chatting with someone. He looked around the place. There was no sign of Janeen.

He shrugged and walked to the counter to sit down when he glanced in the mirror behind the counter and saw that the men were talking to Janeen. Everybody seemed to be having a great old time, chatting and laughing.

Why me, Lord?

He left the counter and walked over to the booth. "Afternoon, George, Harold," he said, pausing beside the booth. They blocked the entrance into the seat across from her. "Excuse me," he said, gently moving Harold out of the way and sliding into the seat.

Janeen looked flushed and her eyes twinkled. He'd never thought of eyes that way but darn if she didn't have the most expressive eyes.

"You know this little lady?" George asked.

Jordan removed his hat and laid it beside him. He shook his head. "Nope. Never saw her before in my life," he said without cracking a smile.

She lifted her brows slightly but made no comment.

"Well," George said, "then I suggest you keep moving along 'cause we want to get better acquainted. Right, Harold?"

Harold nodded, a big grin on his face.

"She's from New York City," George added.

Patsy, the waitress, showed up to say, "Coffee, Jordan?"

"Sounds good. How about one of your great hamburgers, Patsy. I'm going into withdrawal."

"Sure." She jotted something down on her order pad and looked at Janeen. "Would you like something besides your coffee?"

Janeen hesitated and after a moment said, "Do you have chef's salads?"

"Yes, ma'am."

"Good. I'll have one, please."

Harold spoke up. "She's watching her girlish figure."

George laughed. "Well, honey, why don't you let us do that?"

Jordan had had enough. "Okay, guys. Fun's over. Ms. White and I are going to eat before heading back to the ranch."

The men blinked in surprise and looked at each other. "I thought you said—" Harold began.

Jordan cut him off. "It was a joke, Harold. Ms. White is staying at the ranch for a while."

George cleared his throat and in what he thought was a quiet voice blurted out, "Uh-oh. Guess Cindy's not too pleased about that!"

Janeen took a sip of coffee and watched him with interest. Damn, if he didn't blush like some silly schoolgirl. "I'm sure that won't be a problem." He knew it wouldn't be a problem, but he wasn't going to go into detail with these two yahoos.

Patsy returned and refilled their cups. Once she left, Jordan looked at Janeen and in a pleasant voice asked, "Did you find some reading material?"

She held up a bag that looked as though it contained some magazines and books. "Yes. Thank you."

George and Harold wandered off, waved goodbye to Patsy and left the café. As soon as they were gone, Jordan leaned toward Janeen and said, "That sort of flirting is probably routine in New York City," he said, enunciating carefully, "but out here, you can get into trouble real quick. You might want to cool your jets while you're here."

Her back stiffened. "Flirting! I wasn't flirting with anyone."

He nodded. "Uh-huh. So those two just happened to wander over here out of the blue and start talking to you, did they?"

"Not that I owe you any explanations, but when I came in, Patsy saw me and suggested I take a booth, which I did. I ordered coffee, and when she brought it, she commented that I must be new in town. I told her I was visiting from New York. Those men were in the next booth and must have heard me. When they got up, they came over and started talking to me." Her voice had grown icier with each word. "For your information, I don't flirt."

"Right. You just flash those big blue eyes, use your come-hither smile and have men dropping like flies."

All right. So he was losing it a little, but the last thing he needed in his life was Janeen White with her sexy clothes and fancy perfume reminding him of a part of his life he'd long forgotten. Or so he'd thought.

Patsy showed up with the hamburger and salad. Janeen thanked her with a smile, picked up her fork and gave him a look that clearly expressed her displeasure before she began to eat.

Jordan figured he'd said all he needed to say for the next few hours.

Three

Jordan waited to call Cindy until Janeen went to her room. He'd spent the evening in his office catching up with paperwork and was more than ready to stop. Once he heard her bedroom door close, he picked up the phone.

As soon as Cindy answered, he asked, "How's your dad?"

"Oh, hi, Jordan. He's doing a little better today. I told him he was going to see the doctor tomorrow if I had to tie him up and throw him into the back of his truck. So what's been going on with you?"

"You wouldn't believe it," he said with a weariness that had nothing to do with his lack of sleep last night. He leaned back in his chair and propped his boots on the desk.

She chuckled. "That bad, huh?"

"Worse. Jake called me this morning to say that Lindsey had brought her children and a friend of hers to the ranch just in time to be exposed to Joey, who has broken out with chicken pox. So he asked me to let her friend stay here for a few days until they find out if the others are going to catch them."

"Sounds like a good plan to me. Does he like to ride?"

"It's a woman, Cindy. Her name is Janeen White. She's from New York and this is her first visit to Texas. So I'm what you'd consider babysitting her for a few days."

Cindy laughed. "You're joking."

"Wish I was."

"Tell me about her."

After a pause, he said, "I don't know much about her, really. I've been busy since she got here, so I haven't spent much time with her."

"Sounds like you have your hands full."

"You could say that. Do you think you could come by sometime tomorrow—after the doctor's appointment—and meet her? She was asking about you."

"She was?"

"Well, she'd heard about the engagement the other night at the barbecue."

"I'll see what I can do to help out, Jordan."

"I knew I could count on you."

"Okay. Then I'll see you sometime tomorrow. Probably in the afternoon."

"Sounds good."

He hung up, feeling better about the whole thing. He knew Cindy wouldn't mind helping him. They went back a long way. She probably knew him better than anyone. Theirs was a comfortable relationship with no surprises.

He and Cindy made a great team.

Janeen had trouble falling asleep that night. She kept going over what Jordan had said to her at the café. She'd been attacked for no reason. Was he determined to make her feel as uncomfortable as possible while she was there? If so, he'd accomplished his goal.

Once asleep, she tossed and turned, which she chalked up to sleeping in a strange bed. Then again, she hadn't had any trouble sleeping at Lindsey's and Ashley's homes. She didn't want to admit that she had allowed Jordan to get to her.

Toward morning she fell into a deep sleep…until a loud banging on her bedroom door caused her to bolt upright in bed in shock. She looked around wildly, wondering where she was. As soon as she said, "Who is it?" she remembered that she was staying at Jordan's ranch. She immediately felt like a fool. "Jordan?" she quickly added.

"Yeah," he said brusquely. "If you want to go riding this morning, now's the time."

"Oh. Okay. Be right there."

She jumped out of bed and feverishly began to dress. He could have mentioned that they would be riding this morning before they'd retired for the evening. He'd had plenty of time during the silent ride back to the ranch. Once in the house, she'd excused herself and had gone to her room.

Janeen grabbed her boots and opened the door. She could smell the wonderful scent of fresh coffee. She went into the bathroom and got ready to face the day.

And Jordan.

After pulling on her boots, she prepared herself to walk into the kitchen and face him. She found it anticlimactic to discover he wasn't in the kitchen when she got there. Janeen looked out the window and saw him leading two horses wearing saddles and bridles out of the barn.

She looked at the coffeepot with regret and hurried outside.

The sun hadn't come up, but it was light enough to see that there were several people in and around the barn. When she walked up to Jordan, he was giving instructions to a couple of his men.

He glanced around at her. "You said you knew how to ride?"

"Yes."

"Have you used a western saddle before?"

She shook her head.

He locked his hands together for her to step on. Once she put her foot in his hands, he lifted her as she swung her leg over the saddle.

"Put your feet in the stirrups so I can adjust them."

She followed his instructions—actually his orders—and he tightened the leather. She picked up the reins that were hooked around the saddle horn.

He turned away and vaulted into the other saddle and turned his mount toward a dirt road that headed toward the hills. She caught up with him and looked at the countryside.

Janeen soon forgot her companion as she savored the joy of riding once again. She'd really missed it. She watched the sun come up over the hills and gild everything in the landscape with touches of gold. After riding for several minutes, she turned to Jordan and smiled.

He didn't notice. He stared straight ahead, his hat pulled low over his forehead.

She spotted some deer feeding in the early morning. One of them raised its head and looked at them while the rest kept eating. They seemed used to seeing people on horseback. Once they passed the meadow, the doe went back to feeding.

"Thank you for allowing me to ride with you this morning. It's really beautiful out here."

He glanced at her and then away. "The horses needed the exercise. Shall we pick up the pace?" He followed his words with action, and the horses were soon racing down the dirt road.

Janeen felt exhilarated as the wind rushed past her face. She leaned forward slightly, and her horse responded with more speed. By the time Jordan finally began to slow his horse, Janeen was laughing with pleasure.

The mare she rode seemed to have enjoyed the run as much as she had. She stroked her neck and whispered to her.

Jordan had tried to the best of his ability to ignore the woman riding with him. Now he looked at her—flushed and filled with excitement, her hair slipping out of its topknot—and had a flash of what she might look like making love.

The thought made him furious. This was getting way too complicated for him.

They rode for another half hour before stopping by a stream of water swirling around large pieces of rock as it flowed past. There was grass growing along the edges, and the area was shaded by large trees.

"What a great place to picnic," she said.

Jordan didn't comment. Instead, he dismounted and walked over to her as she struggled to get off the mare. He placed his hands on her waist and set her feet on the ground.

She turned and looked at him. "Thanks."

He nodded an acknowledgment and led the horses to the creek.

"Lindsey mentioned that sometimes these creeks become impassable after rains. I guess the water must drain down from the hills. Have you ever been stranded here on the ranch and couldn't get out?"

"Occasionally."

She looked around her while she expertly pulled her hair back into a tidy knot. "It's hard to imagine, isn't it, after seeing it like this?"

Funny, but his imagination was going crazy at the moment.

He looked away from her and cleared his throat. "We need to start heading back as soon as the horses have had a few minutes to rest."

"All right." She wandered along the creek while the horses drank some water and ate some of the grass. She spun around and looked at him. "I never knew places like this existed. I suppose I've seen photographs, but they didn't come close to capturing the beauty."

"I'm glad you're enjoying it."

"Now that you've seen that I can ride, if I promise to stay on the road, will you allow me to come back on my own?"

He studied her for a minute in silence before slowly nodding his head. "I suppose, although it's still dangerous to be out here alone. Maybe Cindy will have some time to ride out with you."

"Speaking of Cindy, when is the big day?"

He looked at her with a puzzled frown. "What are you talking about?"

"Your wedding. When are you getting married?"

He gazed across the land before saying, "We haven't set a date yet."

"Oh. Have you been engaged long?"

Jordan cupped his hands and helped her mount the mare before answering. As he got on his horse, he replied, "Long enough."

He nudged his horse into a canter and didn't speak to her again.

Well. It was evident that he didn't like personal questions, and she'd exhausted most topics of conversation.

Janeen's horse quickly caught up, and when they reached the barn, she quickly dismounted before Jordan had the opportunity to help her. She reached for the bridle just as Jordan appeared by her side. "I'll take care of the horses," he said curtly and led them into the barn.

Well, she had definitely been dismissed. Now what? She remembered the coffee waiting for her inside and walked toward the house. Some of her muscles were stiffening. As soon as she got some coffee she'd take a long, hot shower.

Janeen stood under the warm water and let it ease her aching muscles. No way did she intend to let Jordan know how much she ached. The truth was that she hadn't been on a horse in a couple years, and her body was bitterly complaining.

She finished her shower, blow-dried her hair, wrapped a towel around her and stepped into the hallway, bouncing off Jordan and almost losing the towel.

Flustered, she said, "Oh! I'm sorry. I didn't know you were in the house."

He stared at her, taking in everything about her, from her hair that fell around her shoulders down to her coral-tipped toes. Absently, he said, "I, uh, I forgot something in my room."

She adjusted her towel, her face blazing with embarrassment. How awkward was this? She stepped around him, went inside her room and closed the door.

Jordan stood there, staring at the closed door. What in the world had caused him to agree to this situation? As though his already unruly response to her wasn't bad enough, now he knew exactly what she looked like almost wearing a skimpy towel.

Her breasts had barely been covered, and he'd had to fight the urge to slide his hand across them in a light caress. Now he was as hard as a rock, which would greatly add to the whispers going on among the men if they saw him in this condition.

He went into his room with a scowl.

Janeen spent the rest of the morning looking through his pantry and freezer. She made up one of her favorite casseroles and put it in the refrigerator. She didn't want a repeat of yesterday's scene at the café. Jordan kept his kitchen well stocked with food. He must do his own cooking, unless Cindy spent time over there.

She thought about Jordan's response to her questions about his wedding. He hadn't sounded shy about answering her. Actually, he'd sounded bored with the subject, which seemed odd to her.

Interesting man, if you liked the tall, silent type. She wondered what he and Cindy had to talk about when they spent time together. She grinned. Who knew? He might prefer action to speech.

Once she was through in the kitchen, Janeen got a carrot from the refrigerator and went out to the pen where the stallion roamed. He had plenty of room with several shade trees to keep him out of the hot sun.

As soon as he saw her coming toward him, he raced around the pen. He stopped some distance away and watched her, his ears back.

Janeen slowly reached the fence and rested her arms on top.

"Hello, beauty," she crooned. "You don't have any reason to trust humans, do you?"

His ears flicked forward and back.

"I brought you something," she said, holding out the carrot.

He shook his head, his mane sliding over his shining body.

"I would love to get to know you better."

He watched her for several minutes. She didn't move. Finally, he took two steps toward her and then stopped.

"Would you like to make a friend?" Her voice remained soft and coaxing.

He raced around the pen again. When he stopped, he was a few feet closer to her than before.

She smiled and knelt, placing the carrot just inside the fence.

He stomped his foot.

"I hope you enjoy your snack." Janeen turned away and walked back to the house. Once on the porch, she watched the stallion mince his way to the carrot. He stopped, and his head jerked up when he heard voices from the barn. He waited and watched the barn for several minutes. When no one appeared, he drew closer to the carrot.

After much hesitation, he nipped it from the ground and began to eat.

She hoped he would get used to her. He was as distant as his owner. She would probably have more luck making friends with the horse.

The young dog joined her that afternoon as she sat on the porch. She needed to ask Jordan her name. So far, hers had been the only friendly face she'd seen since she arrived there.

Janeen rubbed her ears and stroked her back. The dog rolled over in a bid for a belly rub, her tail thumping a quick cadence.

Eventually, she rolled onto her side and sighed with contentment. Before long, she was asleep, once again lightly snoring.

Janeen had brought a magazine from her room to read while sitting there. The day was cloudy, and there was a nice breeze blowing. Once in a while she would see one of the men working with one of the horses. She found the horses' responses fascinating.

She'd been outside for a couple hours when she heard the sound of a vehicle coming toward the house. She looked up and watched an older model pickup truck stop in the driveway. A woman got out.

She was tall and rawboned. Her light red hair was pulled back severely from her face, braided and in a coil at the nape of her neck. She wore a green short-sleeved western shirt, faded jeans and well-used boots.

The woman strode toward the porch. When she spotted Janeen, she smiled, showing sparkling white teeth. Janeen stood, ready to explain that Jordan was over around the barn and pastures, but before she could speak, the woman reached her, held out her hand and said, "You must be Janeen. I'm Cindy."

Cindy? As in Jordan's fiancée, Cindy? She was nothing like Janeen had imagined. Janeen took her hand and experienced a firm handshake.

"Sorry I haven't been over earlier," Cindy said. "I guess Jordan told you my dad's been sick so I've been hanging around the house. I finally got him to go to the doctor this morning. I'm hoping the prescribed antibiotics help him."

While she talked, Cindy sat in the rocking chair next to Janeen, who sat back down as well.

"So. Jordan says you're staying here for a few days. Is this your first visit to Texas?"

"Um, yes. I'm visiting my friend, Lindsey Crenshaw. However, the children are under quarantine for a few days at Jake's place. Jordan was kind enough to allow me to stay here."

"Well, that's a bummer. Do you like to ride?"

"Love to. However, Jordan said I can't ride alone."

Cindy nodded sympathetically. "Believe it or not, you can get lost—or at least turned around—on some of these ranches. There's some rough terrain out there. He's trying to keep you safe."

"How kind of him," Janeen replied with a forced smile. "I'm enjoying the peace and quiet here. It's very different from New York."

"I've never been there."

"Maybe Jordan will take you there on your honeymoon," Janeen suggested.

Cindy laughed. "Not likely. Jordan prefers the western side of the Mississippi."

"Jordan mentioned that the two of you haven't set a date to get married."

Cindy made a face. "I know. I guess we should get something lined up. One of these days…" She let her voice fade away.

Janeen didn't know what to say.

Cindy stretched and sighed with contentment. "I'm glad to have a chance to sit for a while. I've really been busy, what with looking after my dad and keeping my training schedule."

"What kind of training do you do?"

Cindy grinned, looking mischievous. "I do barrel racing and stunt riding at local rodeos."

"Really? What kind of stunts?"

"Oh, the usual—riding bareback, hanging off the side of my horse while he's running. I have him stand still while I leap on his back from behind, and I stand on his back while he races around the arena. We seem to be a crowd-pleaser, particularly with the children."

"Is there a chance I can see you at one of the rodeos?"

"You don't have to wait until then. I can show you our moves at my place anytime. I have a practice arena."

"Wow. That's so impressive."

"Do you ride?"

"I do. But not stunts and no barrel racing."

Cindy chuckled. "We'll have to go riding soon, if you'd like."

Janeen nodded. "Jordan took me out this morning, and a few of my muscles are letting me know I haven't been using them very much lately."

"Tell me about New York," Cindy said.

Janeen blinked in surprise. "What do you want to know?"

Cindy shrugged. "Do you like living there?"

"Actually, I do. Right at the moment I'm not working, which is why I have the time to come visit here in Texas."

"You're the first person I've met from there." Cindy studied Janeen for a moment, making her uncomfortable.

"Sorry for staring. I'm fascinated by your skin. It looks so soft and smooth." She blushed and rubbed her cheek self-consciously. "I'm outdoors so much that my face really takes a beating."

"There are things you can put on your skin that will help it." She studied Cindy's face. Cindy's eyes were the color of jade. With her long, thick eyelashes and beautiful smile, she could really look stunning with very little effort.

"Really? I know I'm nothing much to look at. That's probably why…" Her voice trailed off. "Never mind."

Janeen wondered if Cindy was afraid of losing Jordan. It takes all kinds, of course, but she wouldn't want to marry someone who was so casual about getting married. She felt sorry for Cindy.

Jordan was a jerk, in her estimation, despite Lindsey's praises of him. Maybe she should encourage Cindy to transform herself and shake up Mr. Jordan Crenshaw.

Impulsively, she said, "Let's go inside, and I'll show you some of the things I use." It might be fun to teach Cindy a little about skin care.

Cindy grinned. "Okay. I'd like that."

During the next hour, Janeen showed Cindy how to use a specially formulated cleanser, had her put on a mask and when that was washed off, how to use a moisturizing cream.

By the time they finished, Cindy's skin was glowing.

She stood in front of the bathroom mirror in amazement. "Wow. What a difference that makes."

"Would you like to go into town and get some of these products? I noticed the drugstore has a nice selection."

Cindy's eyes sparkled. "I'd love it. Let's do it."

Janeen felt a sense of satisfaction as they started to town. She would do whatever she could to get Jordan to recognize Cindy's beauty. Maybe that would get him to think about setting a date for their wedding.

Four

Once they returned from town, Cindy dropped off Janeen at Jordan's with a promise to see her the next day.

Janeen had enjoyed herself immensely. Cindy had confided that she'd never tried to wear cosmetics because she didn't know what to choose for herself or how to apply it. The one time she had experimented with makeup—as a teenager—her dad told her she looked like a rodeo clown. Since then, Cindy had never worn anything.

Janeen had promised that she would show Cindy how to apply makeup so that it would look natural. Cindy had been dubious but willing to try.

Just as Janeen put her casserole in the oven, she heard her cell phone ringing. She hurried down the hall to her room, where she'd left her purse.

"H'lo?"

"How're you doing today?" Lindsey asked.

"Actually, I've had a busy day. Went riding with Jordan

early this morning—and when I say early, the sun hadn't come up yet—made a casserole for tonight, which I just put in the oven, and Cindy came over to visit this afternoon."

"Oh! What's she like?"

"I don't know what I was expecting, but she surprised me. She's been surrounded by males all her life, so I guess it's natural that she walks, talks and acts like one of the guys. She actually seemed hungry for some female company. We went into town and got a few cosmetics this afternoon, and she said she'd be back tomorrow so I can show her how to use them."

"So you've adopted her as a little sister, have you?"

Janeen laughed. "Not so little. She's half a head taller than I am. But you're right. I can't help but feel sorry for her. Jordan obviously takes her for granted. I mean, I'm sure he must have noticed when she drove up but he didn't bother to come over to say hello, must less show any affection for her."

"No kidding."

"The sad part is that she seems to have accepted his casualness. She's waiting for him to set a date for their wedding, and he acts as though it's no big deal. I think he needs a swift boot in the butt for treating her that way."

"What does she look like?" Lindsey asked.

"Well, she's tall—as I mentioned—slender, with light red hair that's probably been somewhat bleached by the sun. Her green eyes are surrounded by thick, long lashes, but they're too light to really show up, and she has a gorgeous smile. She appears easygoing, which I guess she would have to be to put up with Jordan."

"So all she really needs is some tutoring about girly stuff, huh?"

"That's what I think."

"How's Jordan treating you?"

"Shall I answer politely or truthfully?"

"Uh-oh. That doesn't sound good. Let's go for the truth."

"He's rude and inconsiderate and that's when he's on his best behavior. I guess he can't help being gruff. You already warned me that he isn't one to socialize. I'm sure he's doing his best. He took me to town yesterday to get something to read while I'm here, which he didn't have to do, and bought me supper while we were in town." She didn't want to go into detail about that. "How are things going over there?"

"Actually, the kids are being better than I expected, which makes me a little nervous. Mine aren't complaining, but they aren't very energetic, which is most unusual."

"You think maybe they've caught Joey's chicken pox?"

"It's too soon to tell but I'm beginning to suspect so. Heather's helping to entertain them. She's a teenager now and very close to Ashley, who tells me that Heather makes very little effort to see her mother."

"Who could blame her? Dropping her off on her father who didn't know she existed before that night had to have been traumatic for her, regardless of her young age."

"Well, she's a godsend now, that's for sure."

Janeen paused and then said, "I hear someone in the kitchen. It's probably Jordan. Thanks for checking on me. Keep me posted on how everything develops over there, okay?"

"No problem. Bye."

"Take care," she said and put down her phone. When she looked up, she saw that Jordan had paused in front of her door.

As soon as she looked at him, he said, "Boyfriend missing you?"

She wanted to roll her eyes at the question but managed to refrain. "Why, of course he is. He can't eat, can't sleep. He's pining away for me. However, that was Lindsey checking in with me."

Jordan's ears turned red. "Look, I, uh, need to get cleaned up, and then we'll think about supper."

"I have a casserole in the oven that should be ready by the time you finish with your shower."

He looked at her with surprise. "Oh. Well. Thanks."

"You're welcome." Once she heard his bedroom door close, she shook her head. He was a mystery but not one she wanted to waste time solving.

Jordan closed the bedroom door behind him and then stood there, leaning against it. She'd made something for them to eat? That was the last thing he would have imagined someone like her would do.

He gave his head a shake and went in to take a shower. Maybe he'd go spend the evening with Cindy. He could let his guard down and relax with her. He enjoyed her company. Maybe it was time to start making plans for a wedding.

Janeen woke up early the next day. Not that she expected to ride again but she wanted to enjoy the early morning. Jordan had left coffee for her. After she poured a cup, she went outside and stood on the porch. The air smelled fresh, and the view of the sun coming up, touching everything with a warm, golden glow, made her sigh with pleasure.

As usual, there were several men in and around the barn. Jordan was probably one of them.

She had to give him credit. He'd been very polite while they ate the night before, insisting on cleaning up the kitchen once they finished. He excused himself later to say he was going to see Cindy, which made the relationship seem more normal. Let's face it; she'd had no reason to think their love for each other wasn't deep-seated. No doubt each couple's relationship was different.

Besides, how would she know? She'd never been engaged. Never been close to considering marriage, despite everything her mother had tried to do to get her married off to a son of any number of her friends.

Actually, she was glad for this time of reflection. She wasn't certain if she wanted to work in a museum anymore. She'd trained in the field, but maybe it was time to think about a change.

Hopefully by the time she returned home, she'd have a handle on what she wanted to do with the rest of her life.

Janeen stayed outside after she finished her coffee. Oh, how she wished she could ride this morning. Of course she understood Jordan's reluctance to let her go alone. At least she could go down and visit the horses.

Janeen made some toast and cleaned up the kitchen before she found a couple of carrots in the vegetable bin and headed toward the barn. Halfway there, she saw the black stallion watching her.

She veered to walk toward him. He watched her come closer, his ears twitching. When she stood beside the fence, he whiffed at her. She didn't move. He took several steps back and snorted. He shook his head, his mane flowing along his neck.

She remained still. Finally, she said softly, "Good morning, fella."

His ears flickered and he moved restlessly, not taking his eyes off her.

"You look lonesome over here by yourself." As soon as she spoke, his ears went forward, watching her warily...but he stayed where he was. "I know. You have a very good reason not to trust people." She leaned against the fence. When she did, he whirled away and ran back to the other side of the corral. He had a beautiful stride, she noted.

Janeen held out a carrot. "I'm going to leave this for you," she said, kneeling to place a carrot on the grass through the boards of the fence. She stood and nodded, deliberately turning her back on him, and walked away. After several steps, she turned slightly to see what he was doing. He'd moved back to the middle of the pasture, his head extended toward the carrot.

She smiled and continued into the barn.

The sun's rays hadn't entered the barn yet, and the overhead lights glowed brightly. One of the men paused while cleaning out a stall and looked at her. She smiled at him. "Good morning," she said.

He dipped his head. "Mornin', ma'am," he muttered and continued to work. She took her time looking into each stall, stroking the nose of any horse that was there, until she spotted Jordan in one of the stalls checking a horse's hooves.

"Another beautiful day, isn't it?" she asked, determined to be friendly and polite if it killed her.

He glanced up and blinked at her in surprise. "You're up early." Without his hat, his hair looked messy, as though he had a habit of running his hand through it.

"This is my favorite time of day," she said in reply, giving him the benefit of the doubt as to why he made the comment.

He lowered the hoof and straightened. "That surprises me."

"Why?"

He shrugged. "You don't seem the type."

She took a deep breath, no longer giving him the benefit of believing he was being polite. She rested one hand on her hip and asked, "And what type is that?" She'd hang on to her smile if it killed her.

He gave his head a quick shake. "Don't mind me."

"No, really. I'd like to know what type you think I am."

"I don't know you well enough to form an opinion about you."

"That hasn't seemed to stop you since I've been here, though."

He ran his fingers through his hair and looked at her. She could see that he was uncomfortable. Now he knew how she felt when he did the same to her.

"The thing is," he began and then fell silent.

She waited him out.

"I don't know all that many women who live in large cities. I just figured your lifestyle is a lot different from mine."

She crossed her arms. "Well, you do have a point there. It's true I don't ride a horse down Fifth Avenue, and the predators there are generally human and not wildlife. However, when I was working I was up by five every morning in order to get to work on time."

They stared at each other in silence. Eventually, Janeen left the barn and went back to the house before she said anything caustic. She had to ignore his boorishness since she needed to stay here. Otherwise, she might cause him bodily injury. She doubted that Cindy would approve.

Jordan watched her leave the barn and felt as if he'd barely managed to sidestep a minefield. She was definitely angry, but she'd managed to keep her cool, whereas he came off as being a real ass. He supposed he couldn't really blame her for being angry at him. Just because he was physically attracted to her didn't mean he had to take his frustrations out on her.

The problem was that if he dropped the tight rein he had over his behavior when he was around her, he was afraid of what he might say or—worse—do. The scene in the café was a good example of him overreacting to a situation where she was involved. He'd felt like a fool when it was all over and she'd never said another word to him for the rest of the evening.

It didn't help any that Cindy thought so much of her. Most of his time at Cindy's last night was spent listening to her rave on about Janeen. He didn't really follow all the stuff she'd talked about—something about a makeover, whatever the hell that was—but he hadn't seen Cindy that animated before.

At least Cindy would keep Janeen occupied and out of his hair. Right now, that was the best he could hope for.

He really hoped she'd be leaving soon. His grip on his self-control wouldn't last much longer.

Five

Cindy arrived a little after nine. She tapped on the screen door of the kitchen just as Janeen filled a cup with coffee.

"Just in time for coffee, if you'd like some," she said, smiling.

Cindy shook her head. "None for me, thanks." She looked away, not meeting Janeen's eyes. "I hope I'm not too early."

"Not at all."

"The thing is, I'm not sure if this makeup thing is really going to work for me. I mean, I'm more comfortable in jeans and riding horses than trying to look like something I'm not."

Janeen studied the woman. Her eyes…and her smile…were her best features. However, Janeen didn't want to push Cindy into doing something she wasn't ready to do.

"You know you look fine the way you are, Cindy," she finally said.

Cindy bobbed her head in agreement. "It's just that…" She stopped. Janeen waited. Finally, Cindy continued, "I guess what I'm saying is that no matter what I do I'm not going to look like a sophisticated city woman."

"Why would you want to?"

Cindy shrugged. Then she burst out, "I'm just tired of being treated like one of the guys. I want to do something to make them see me differently."

"Like Jordan?" Janeen asked with a smile.

Cindy looked startled for a second before she said, "Uh, yeah. Jordan. Of course." Her cheeks turned red.

Janeen wasn't sure what was going on. "So do you want to try the makeup and see what you think?"

She looked uncertain. "I guess it wouldn't hurt to try it once."

"True."

Cindy relaxed. "After we do that, I wondered if you'd like to go over to my place, and I'll show you my horses and some of the things they can do. Maybe we could ride around, and I could show you our place."

"Sounds like fun." Being on her own playing field, so to speak, might help Cindy have more confidence in herself.

Cindy stuck her hands in the back pockets of her jeans. "So what now?" she asked.

Janeen rubbed her hands together and chuckled wickedly. "And now, my pretty, I will teach you some magical tricks."

Cindy blushed. "It will take magic, believe me."

Janeen took one of the kitchen chairs, carried it to her bedroom and placed it in front of the dresser mirror.

Cindy looked around the room and grimaced. "Not much in the way of decorations in here, are there?"

"I don't mind. I was sort of pushed onto Jordan to stay here. I'm comfortable enough."

For the next hour, the two of them talked about makeup and when and how and why to use it. By the time they finished, Cindy could scarcely believe what the mirror reflected. "Is that really me?"

Janeen admitted to herself that Cindy looked even better than she had hoped when she started this project. Jordan would definitely be impressed with her transformation.

"It doesn't look as though I'm wearing makeup at all," Cindy murmured, brushing her fingers lightly across her cheek. She glanced at Janeen in the mirror. "I'm not sure I'll be able to do it on my own."

"You'll be surprised at how easy it becomes with practice. Now then, why don't we go to your place, and you can show me what barrel racing is."

Cindy stood slowly, still staring into the mirror. Then she turned and nodded. "You bet. Let's go."

They were on the porch, ready to leave, when they heard the sound of a truck pulling into the yard. As soon as Cindy saw who it was, she dropped her head and looked away.

Janeen watched as a long-legged cowboy got out of a dark blue truck. The dogs came running out of the barn to greet him. "I've been meaning to ask Jordan the names of the dogs, but I keep forgetting."

"The older one that follows Jordan everywhere is Gus. The younger one is Feisty."

Janeen laughed and watched the man enter the barn. She glanced at Cindy. "Do you know who that is?"

"Sure," she replied, sounding casual. "All of us grew up together. He and Jordan's brother, Jack, travel around the country entering rodeos together. I didn't know he was in town."

Janeen studied her in silence for a moment. "What's his name?" she finally asked.

"Mark."

Something had changed in Cindy since Mark had arrived. She was much more reserved than she'd been earlier. Janeen wondered why.

"I guess you know him well, then."

Cindy lifted one shoulder in a slight shrug. "Yeah, I guess so."

"I get the feeling you don't like him."

Cindy looked startled before she shrugged and said, "What's not to like? He's the epitome of tall, dark and handsome...a walking cliché." After a moment, Cindy added, "He's always treated me like one of the guys." She smiled ruefully. "And why shouldn't he? Everyone else does."

Janeen chuckled. "Well, honey, I have a hunch that no one is going to mistake you for one of the guys now. You look great."

As though making up her mind about something, Cindy straightened her shoulders. "Come on. Let's go out there. I'll introduce you."

Janeen wasn't certain why Cindy felt the need to have her meet the guy. However, she went along with it.

"Okay."

Cindy ran her hand over her hair in a self-conscious gesture as they left the porch. Janeen noticed that the black stallion raised his head and looked at them as they walked toward the barn.

"Hold on. I'll be back in a minute," she said and went back into the kitchen for a carrot. When she rejoined Cindy, Cindy looked at the carrot with a puzzled expression.

"You hungry?"

Janeen chuckled. "No. I want to give this to the stallion."

"Better be careful around him."

"Oh, I'm not going to crawl into his pen. I'll just leave the carrot where he can reach it."

The stallion watched them closely as they approached the fence. He spun around and trotted to the other side of the pen and turned to watch them. He stomped one of his forelegs and made a huffing noise.

"Good morning to you, beauty," Janeen said when she reached the fence. She waited patiently, and eventually the stallion minced slowly to the middle of the pen. "Thought you might enjoy another treat." She leaned down and put the carrot in the same place she'd put the others and stepped away. Without waiting to see what he would do, she rejoined Cindy and they continued to the barn.

When they walked inside, Janeen saw the two men talking a few stalls away. Jordan saw them and said, "Hi, ladies. Janeen, let me introduce you to a friend of mine. This is Mark Shepard."

"Hi, Mark. I'm Janeen White. Jordan has been kind enough to allow me to stay here for a few days."

Mark held out his hand and flashed a killer grin. "He was just telling me about you." Mark Shepard was definitely tall, with dark hair and eyes, and strikingly handsome. Wow, he was something else.

She took his hand and felt the calluses. "Do you live in the area?"

"Grew up here. I follow the rodeo circuit with Jordan's brother, Jack. I try to stop in whenever I get the chance." He glanced at Cindy. "Hey, Cindy, how's it going?"

"Fine." She stood with her hands in the back pockets of her jeans.

Janeen waited for one of the men to say something about Cindy's new look, but neither of them seemed to notice.

"Jack mentioned that you and Jordan got engaged, Cindy," Mark said. He winked at Jordan. "And here you were a confirmed bachelor."

Janeen watched Cindy, who seemed to be uncomfortable. Why? Was it because Jordan hadn't really looked at her since they arrived? She glanced at Jordan and was surprised to see that he was watching her, a muscle jumping in his jaw.

"That's right," he said, without taking his eyes off Janeen.

Mark spoke, and Janeen realized he was talking to her. "I hope Jordan has been showing you around the area. He said you're from New York."

"That's right."

"I'll be glad to volunteer my services." He glanced back at Jordan. "Say. I've got a great idea. Why don't we take these gals out for some dinner and dancing tomorrow night? I've already made plans for tonight, otherwise we could do it earlier. We'll show Janeen how Texans like to celebrate weekends. She won't find anything like this back in New York."

Jordan frowned and then looked at Cindy. "Would you like to do that, Cindy?"

"I guess." She glanced at Janeen. "I think it's time for you to see a little Texas nightlife, don't you?"

"Oh. Well, then, I guess I'm all right with the idea."

Mark smiled. "Great." He walked over to one of the stalls, nodded his head at the mare and asked Jordan a question. They were soon deep in discussion about horses as though the women weren't there.

Janeen smiled and said, "I guess we've been dismissed."

Cindy turned away and briskly walked toward the door. She waited until they reached the truck. "So much for wowing them with my new look. Neither one noticed."

"Well, then, this calls for more drastic measures. Just wait until tomorrow night. Let's go shopping in Austin, and we'll set them both on their collective ear."

"You, maybe. But not me. They know me so well they never really look at me."

"Believe me, honey, they will both look at you tomorrow night."

Six

The drive to Cindy's home took forty-five minutes. The distances Texans took for granted continued to amaze Janeen. When they turned at the entrance, Janeen noticed the stonework and wrought iron that gave the place a great look.

"How long have you lived here?" she asked.

They drove over a cattle guard. "All my life. The ranch has been in the family for years."

"Like the Crenshaws."

Cindy smiled. "Oh, our place is nothing like theirs. It's tough to make a living at ranching. You have to love it to want to stay here. It's all about long hours, backbreaking work and dealing with all kinds of weather. Like I said, you have to really love the lifestyle."

"And you do, I take it?"

Cindy shrugged. "It's all I know." She pulled up in front of a large house and stopped. "Here we are."

Janeen looked around as she got out of the truck. The house

was one story with vinyl siding and a metal roof. A porch stretched across the front of it and disappeared around a corner.

Flowering bushes framed the porch. "This is beautiful, Cindy."

"Thanks. Our foreman's wife keeps up with the gardening. Everything I try to grow dies. She once said I need to practice benign neglect when gardening. I tend to overwater, overfertilize, over-everything." She stuck her hands in her back pockets. "Let's go see my horses."

"Sounds good."

They walked across the drive to a barn. It was much smaller than Jordan's. Regardless, it was a nice size, and when they walked inside, she saw several stalls. Cindy walked to the other end of the barn and opened a wide gate. They stepped inside and Janeen looked around.

Five horses were moving toward them. "They're beautiful," she said, admiring their glossy coats.

Cindy walked over to a reddish-brown horse. "This is Molly," she said, draping her body against the horse's side. "She's helped me win a great many barrel races."

"How does a race like that work?"

"You're judged by the time it takes you to run a course similar to the one I have set up in the next pasture."

Janeen looked at the barrels lined up in a row. "You have to ride between them?"

"Yep. It calls for complete trust between horse and rider. If you touch one of the barrels, you're disqualified. Would you like to see Molly and I in action?"

"I'd love it."

Janeen had grown up watching steeplechase races, but this was something new to her. As the hours went by, she gained a great deal of respect for Cindy's abilities. She was glad she'd come. Here was a confident, talented Cindy, relaxed and happy. Janeen could see why Cindy and Jordan would make a go of their marriage.

She helped Cindy bring the horses back to their stalls, feed and water them, while Cindy brushed and cooled down Molly. They were walking out of the barn when Jordan drove up.

"Evenin'," he said with a smile. He walked over to Cindy and put his arm around her shoulders, giving her a hug. "What did you think of Cindy's riding?" he asked, looking at Janeen.

"I'm in awe of her talent." She noticed that Cindy blushed. She really was pretty with her hair slipping out of her braid, curling around her face, and her eyes sparkling. They looked good together.

"I thought I might take you ladies to dinner," he said.

"Not necessary," Cindy replied. "I've had a slow cooker on all day with a pot roast and vegetables. There's enough for everybody."

Jordan kissed Cindy's cheek. "Sounds good to me."

Once inside, Janeen met Cindy's dad, who was setting the table. He already had four place settings out.

Janeen watched the dynamics of the three, smiling at how close Jordan seemed to be to Cindy's father.

She felt like she was seeing Jordan for the first time: relaxed, laughing and teasing Cindy. He actually seemed like a decent guy.

All of that changed once they got into his truck to go back to his place. After waving goodbye and driving away, he didn't say anything at all to Janeen. He couldn't have made it any clearer to her that she was a nuisance to him.

Their ride home was in silence.

Cindy picked up Janeen around seven the next morning, and they headed out to Austin.

"What did you do after you went home last night?" Cindy asked once they were on the highway heading northeast.

"Not much. Watched a little TV and then went to bed."

"Did Jordan watch with you?" Cindy asked, her tone deliberately casual.

Uh-oh. Please don't let her be jealous of me, of all people.

"He was shut up in his office all evening. Why?"

"I just wondered." A few miles later, she said, "Sometimes I get the feeling I'm invisible."

"Because Jordan didn't notice that you had done something different to your appearance yesterday?"

Cindy nodded.

Janeen wasn't sure what to say to reassure her since she was afraid Cindy was right. Finally, she said. "He already knows you're beautiful. Maybe he had something on his mind."

"Me, beautiful? Hah. Nobody sees me as a woman. It didn't used to bother me, but now that I've met you, I guess I want to explore my feminine side...if I even have one."

"Maybe you don't see your beauty, but I certainly do. If you want to get Jordan's attention, I have a few suggestions."

"I'm open to anything you suggest."

"Okay. Let's plan our day."

As soon as they reached the city, Cindy drove to one of the malls. Once inside, Janeen paused and looked at Cindy. "Are you sure you want to do this? I don't want to talk you into doing something you might later regret."

"I want to do it."

"All right." They looked at the directory and found a hair salon. Janeen was relieved to see a sign that said "walk-ins welcome," since they didn't have an appointment.

As soon as one of the women came up and asked if she could help them, Cindy said, "Yes, please. I want to have my hair cut and styled."

The young woman said, "Okay. Let's get started."

Once she finished, the woman held a mirror for Cindy to look at her hair from different angles.

"I can't believe it," Cindy whispered, staring into the mirror.

"It's beautiful," Janeen said. It certainly was. The haircut and styling did wonders for Cindy. With the weight off, her hair fell in soft waves around her face and down to her shoulders. The conditioner the beautician used made Cindy's hair look luxurious.

Cindy touched the hair that feathered across her forehead. She looked in the mirror at Janeen's reflection. "I love it."

"Good."

Cindy paid the woman, and then they went back out into the mall. "Now what?"

"I have an idea. Let's go into one of these department stores and see if we can get you a facial. They'll show you what cosmetics you need much better than I did. They have more of a selection of colors and shades than the drugstore has."

After the session with cosmetics, they went to the food court to eat. Janeen was amused that Cindy was unaware of the looks she was getting from the males she passed.

The layered hairdo framing her face brought attention to her beautiful eyes. There was no way that Jordan wouldn't notice and react to her now.

After lunch they stopped at a few boutiques and department stores to look at clothes.

"I have no idea what to buy. I'm overwhelmed by all the choices."

"All right. First, look for the colors you like to wear. Then I'll pick a few outfits for you to try on. Let me know the ones you like, and we can go from there."

Once Cindy found a few things she liked, they shopped for shoes. Janeen stressed that comfort would be what to look for and then style.

By the time they gathered all the things Cindy had bought it was almost four o'clock.

"Can you believe that we've spent the entire day at the mall?" Cindy asked, sounding incredulous. "I practically have a brand-new wardrobe."

"I told you that you're beautiful. Now do you believe me?"

Cindy chuckled. "Well, I'll never win a beauty pageant but I look a heck of a lot better than I did." Cindy had changed into one of the outfits she'd bought: a sleeveless white blouse and light green slacks. She wore sandals now instead of her boots.

She chattered all the way home. "I'm so glad we're going out tonight. I think they'll—I mean *he*—will really be surprised."

"You can count on it."

When they reached Jordan's ranch, Janeen hopped out of the truck and waved goodbye to Cindy.

She had just stepped onto the porch when the kitchen door opened and a frowning Jordan greeted her.

"Where the heck have you been all day!"

She continued into the house, forcing him to step out of the way. Once inside, she turned and looked at him.

"I was with Cindy."

"Well, you could have left a note or something. I'm supposed to be looking after you, and it's more than a little difficult to do when I have no idea where you are."

"You could have called me if you were concerned," she said quietly.

Still frowning, Jordan replied, "I don't have your number."

She walked over to the phone, took a pad and pen and wrote down her cell-phone number. She handed it to him.

"Did you two forget that we're supposed to meet Mark for dinner?"

She smiled. "We remembered."

She suddenly noticed that he was cleaned up, wearing nice slacks, black boots and a red western-cut shirt. "I see you're ready to go."

"Just waiting for you."

"I won't be long," she replied and went into her room.

Janeen looked through the clothes she'd brought with her from Houston. She finally settled on a sundress she'd found during a shopping expedition with Lindsey several days ago. It was soft green and had spaghetti straps. It fit snugly to her waist, where it flared out into a skirt that ended at her knees. She hoped her choice was acceptable. She'd been invited for dinner, after all. And dancing. She was curious about what Cindy would choose to wear. Cindy hadn't decided when she'd dropped Janeen off.

Whatever she chose, Janeen knew that Jordan Crenshaw would definitely notice his fiancée tonight.

As soon as she saw Jordan, she knew she'd done something wrong. He'd been waiting in the living room, watching news, when he glanced up and saw her. His frown was ferocious. Now what?

"What's wrong?" she finally asked, when he stood and walked toward her. "Should I wear something else?"

"Probably wouldn't make any difference," he muttered. "Let's go."

As soon as they stepped outside and walked across the porch, the wind swirled around the house, ballooning her skirt. She quickly grabbed the front before reaching to catch the back. The wind tugged and cavorted around her as though determined to make her fight for her modesty.

When the breeze finally died back down, she hurried down the steps. Jordan was already at his truck, holding the passenger-side door open. She hurried over to him. "I'm sorry. I was having a bit of trouble with the wind and—"

He closed the door as he said, "Yeah, I saw."

In fact, he'd seen much more than he'd ever wanted to see again of Ms. Janeen White's long, shapely legs, and he could have gone on for the rest of his life without needing to know that her panties matched the color of her dress.

He got into the truck and started the engine. What a fun evening this was going to be. Hopefully, Mark would keep Janeen occupied and away from him. He rubbed his forehead.

"Do you have a headache? I have some aspirin that might help," she asked.

He shook his head. He had an ache all right, but nothing he'd discuss with her. He didn't think an aspirin would make it go away.

Once again, they rode in silence until they reached Cindy's home.

Jordan pulled up and went inside to get Cindy. He left the truck running so that Janeen would have some air-conditioning.

He nodded to Cindy's dad. "Is Cindy ready?"

Her father answered with another question. "Have you seen Cindy today?"

"Uh, no, I haven't. Isn't she here?"

"Oh, she's here, all right. Almost didn't recognize my own daughter."

Alarmed, Jordan asked, "Has she been hurt?" Why hadn't Janeen said something if she'd been injured in some way?

"You'll see for yourself." He raised his voice, "Jordan's here, honey."

"I'll be right there."

When she walked into the living room, Jordan gave her a quick glance. "You ready to go?" He paused and added, "You look nice tonight."

"Thanks."

As they walked out the door, he asked, "Did you do something to your hair?"

"Had it cut."

She turned around to face him. The dress she had on was sleeveless, and the black material crossed over her breasts, calling attention to them. The rest of the dress fit snugly. It stopped just below her knees.

They paused on the porch. Jordan frowned. "Can you walk in that thing?"

"Of course," she replied. "See the slit on the side?" She moved toward the steps, and the dress parted to mid-thigh. "Do you like it?"

He shrugged, escorting her to his truck. "Yeah, I guess. You don't really look like you," he mumbled.

"Janeen helped me pick out some things."

Oh, hell. So this was all Janeen's idea, was it? Wouldn't he just know she'd pull something like this! He'd liked Cindy the way she was, although he had to admit the haircut looked good. And when had she started wearing lipstick?

When they reached his truck, Jordan noticed that Janeen had

gotten into the back. He walked Cindy around to the passenger side, opened the door, scooped her up into her arms, causing her to squeal in surprise, and placed her on the seat.

"There's no way you'd be able to get into the truck without showing your...showing everything."

Cindy looked around at Janeen and winked.

"You look fabulous," Janeen said.

Well, of course she does. What's that got to do with anything? He liked her just the way she'd been! He got back into the truck, slammed the door and started driving to town.

"Where did we decide to eat?" Cindy asked.

"El Sombrero. Thought we'd show Janeen what real Tex-Mex food is all about."

Cindy looked around at Janeen. "Hope you don't mind spicy food."

Jordan looked into the rearview mirror and saw Janeen sitting behind him. Damn, the woman was beautiful. She caught him looking at her and smiled. He jerked his eyes back to the road.

He had a hunch this was going to be a long night.

Seven

Mark was already at the restaurant when they arrived. He spotted them as soon as they drove up and met them at the door. "Well, hello, Ms. White. Aren't you looking nice tonight? I hope you like Mexican food because this place serves the best." He flashed his white grin, which contrasted nicely with his sun-darkened skin.

She looked around the room. The place had Mexican tile floors and adobe-looking walls with sombreros and serapes hanging on them. The place definitely had atmosphere.

Mark nodded toward Jordan. "Glad we could get together. I—" He coughed. "Cindy?" he asked hoarsely.

She smiled. "Hi, Mark."

"Cindy?" he repeated, staring at her as though he'd never seen her before. "I had no idea—" He seemed to be at a loss for words.

"Are you ready to be seated?" the hostess, dressed in a colorful full skirt and off-the-shoulder white blouse, asked.

Jordan stepped forward. "Yes. Thank you."

Jordan placed his hand on Cindy's waist and motioned for her to follow the hostess.

Janeen looked at Mark. "Are you okay?"

"I can't believe it," he said in a low voice. "I had no idea that Cindy O'Neil could look like that. I mean, she looks great in that dress. And her hair. What did she do with her hair?"

Janeen started forward to follow the other couple. "Cut it," she said, walking past him.

Throughout dinner Mark couldn't keep his eyes off Cindy. Janeen glanced at Jordan, wondering if he was bothered. From the way he talked, sipped his beer and ate the combination plate he'd ordered, she didn't think he'd noticed.

Then he looked directly at her, and she realized that she'd been staring at him. She blushed at his straightforward stare. After a moment she went back to her salad.

Each of them did what they could to bring her into the conversation, but she didn't know any of the names or places they discussed. So she sat there and listened and smiled.

When dinner was over, they left. Janeen rode with Mark.

"How do you like being here?" Mark asked, leading the way to the dance hall.

"It's quite an experience."

"How long are you going to stay?"

"At Jordan's? Not very long. I'll probably be leaving the area next week."

"Have you and Cindy made friends?"

"I guess you could say that. I really like her."

"She's been a tomboy all her life. The two of you don't seem to have much in common. She's never bothered dressing up before. That's why it was such a shock to see her looking like a woman." He paused. "That didn't sound right, but you know what I mean."

"How long have you known her?"

"Lordy, I can't remember a time when I didn't know her. She was a couple years behind me in school. I never saw much of her. She was always busy doing something. Have you seen that gal ride?"

"She took me to her place yesterday. She's good."

"She's something else. Totally fearless on the back of that horse. She's got that mare so well trained that she'll do anything for her."

"I can tell that you admire her."

"Well, yeah. I can't see her getting married, though."

"Why not?"

"Guess I'd never given it much thought that she might. She never paid attention to us guys when we were growing up. She's always been more interested in her horses than in men. But to see her like that tonight... Wow. I guess she somehow grew up when I wasn't looking." He thought for a moment or two. "She and Jordan have a lot in common, so I guess it makes sense that they'd end up together."

"So it would seem."

"Do you ride?"

"Yes."

"Been out riding since you got here?"

"A few times."

"Maybe we can get together while I'm in town. Maybe make a day of it."

She wondered if her sore muscles could handle long hours in the saddle. "Do you have any particular place we might go?"

"We can stay on Jordan's ranch and ride back in the hills."

"I think I would enjoy that."

"Good. I'll get back to you when I know which day would work out best for me. I'll bring my own mount. I'm sure Jordan has a horse you can ride."

She smiled. "He has several."

"You got a favorite?"

"Not really. At the present time I'm trying to get the black stallion to accept me."

"That's one horse you can't ride. He's bad news."

"So Jordan said."

Up ahead of them Janeen saw a large neon light on the roof of a huge building that looked as if it could be used for a plane hangar. The place was surrounded by cars.

"Is that where we're going?"

"Yep. Hope you like country music. They have live music on the weekends."

Mark pulled around to the side of the building, with Jordan right behind them. He found two places together and pulled into one of them while Jordan took the other space.

Her door opened and Jordan stood there, holding out his hand. She looked around. Mark and Cindy were already waiting behind the truck.

Janeen put her hand in his and stepped out. He held her by the waist until her feet touched the ground.

"Maybe I should have warned you about the loud music," he said as they joined Mark and Cindy.

"I'm sure I can stand it for a little while," she replied absently, her glance caught by the way Cindy was looking up at Mark. She glowed; there was no other way to describe her. Mark had definitely noticed—and seemed to appreciate—the new Cindy.

There was a line waiting to get inside. From the sounds emanating from the building, there was a crowd already there. Janeen wondered what she'd gotten herself into. Jordan was acting like he was on his way to having teeth pulled without the aid of anesthetic.

Once inside, they found a tall table with four tall chairs. Janeen and Cindy sat while the men went to the bar for their drinks.

Cindy grinned.

"Your eyes are sparkling," Janeen said.

Cindy laughed. "I've never been here before, just like I was never invited to any of the dances when I was in school. I feel like Cinderella."

"Then I'm glad we came."

"Oh, so am I!" Cindy replied fervently. "I keep wantin' to pinch myself to make sure I'm not dreaming."

The men returned with two long-necked bottles of beer and two soft drinks.

"There's some toe-tapping music," Mark said, not sitting down. "Janeen, how about we try to show them how it's done."

She shook her head, laughing. "Oh, no. Not me. I came to watch, not to participate."

Mark looked at Cindy. "How about it, Cindy? You want to dance?" He glanced at Jordan. "You don't mind, do you?" he asked with a grin.

"Not at all," Jordan replied after taking a sip of his beer. "Have fun." He winked at Cindy and smiled.

For some reason that Janeen didn't understand, Cindy blushed a deep red. What was up with that?

The one thing she did understand was that Jordan probably wouldn't talk to her while they sat there so she watched the dancers. The dance floor took up most of the space in the building, its rectangular shape ending at a stage at one end and the bar at the other.

Most of the people on the floor were making a giant circle dancing with their partners as they swirled. Some were doing some sort of line dancing that looked like fun.

Finally, she looked at Jordan and discovered he was staring at her with an intensity that caused her to shiver. She blinked, and the heated expression was gone as though it had never been there.

Probably hadn't, for that matter. The low light around the edges of the dance floor cast shadows at the tables.

"Do you like to dance?" she finally asked.

"Shall I be polite or honest?" he asked with a half smile.

Janeen smiled, having used the same comment a few times herself. "I prefer honesty every time."

"I've never been comfortable making a fool of myself, which I would do if I got out there. I didn't know Cindy liked to dance. She's quite good," he said, nodding to the dance floor.

Janeen watched as Mark spun Cindy out and quickly brought her back to him while they continued to move around the floor. "She looks happy."

"Yeah," he said quietly. "She does."

After another lengthy silence, Jordan sighed and said, "Why don't we get out there and try it. I'll do my best not to step on your toes."

She didn't want to be rude after his magnanimous offer, so she nodded and stepped down to the floor. They were weaving between the crowded tables when the music changed and slowed down. The couples turned to each other and followed the music.

Janeen hesitated, not at all sure that dancing with Jordan was a good idea. She felt his hand at her back as they stepped onto the dance floor. When she turned toward him, Jordan placed his arm around her waist and took her hand in his.

Standing this close, she was aware of the scent of his aftershave. Her head reached his shoulders. After a few steps, Jordan pulled her closer, moving their clasped hands to his chest.

He had lied about not being able to dance. He was smooth and guided her with a firm hand. Janeen caught sight of Mark and Cindy. He had both arms wrapped around her waist, her arms around his neck. Whatever they were talking about seemed to be serious.

Janeen glanced at Jordan to see if he'd noticed.

He hadn't. Instead, he was watching the band.

Jordan knew that deciding to dance with Janeen was the height of stupidity on his part. The woman was driving him crazy. He wished he knew why he reacted so strongly to her.

He recalled when he'd made up his mind to get married. He wanted a family, and he knew and trusted Cindy. They had a great deal in common. He admired and respected her. He'd known her for years, so there wouldn't be any surprises. When he'd suggested to Cindy that they get married, she'd been a little surprised. They talked about the idea. He'd pointed out all the reasons he thought they could make a marriage work. She thought about his offer for a few days and eventually agreed that getting married would offer both of them a chance for a life and family together.

None of that had changed. Unfortunately, all the while he'd tried to talk some sense into his head, his body was busy betraying him. Without realizing it, he'd pulled her closer to him, so that she was pressed against him. He glanced at her, but that didn't help. Her head rested on his shoulder and her eyes were closed.

He could have gone all night without that image.

The music finally stopped, and the band announced they were taking a break. Recorded music came on but Jordan ignored it and led Janeen back to their table where Mark and Cindy waited.

Cindy looked really nice tonight. He'd never noticed her eyes before. They sparkled and her cheeks were flushed. Thank God she seemed to be enjoying herself.

"Hey," Mark said with a grin, "you two looked like you were enjoying yourselves." He looked at Jordan, one eyebrow lifted. "Time to switch partners, don't you think?"

"Let's wait until the band returns," Cindy said with a sigh. "They're great, aren't they?"

Janeen had never seen Cindy so vivacious. She looked great. Nobody would mistake her for one of the guys now. The men stood and Mark said, "We're doing a beer run. Any takers?"

Janeen shook her head. "None for me, thanks."

"One for me, please," Cindy replied.

Once they were out of earshot, Cindy leaned over. "I can't remember a time when I've so enjoyed myself. Mark keeps talking about how I look."

"For good reason."

Cindy laughed. "He said I cleaned up quite nicely."

"You've just added a little pizzazz to your appearance, that's all. No one could expect you to dress like that at a rodeo."

Cindy nodded, suddenly quiet. "Mark asked if I wanted to go follow the circuit with him."

"How do you feel about that?"

"I'm not sure. I don't think Jordan would like that very much."

Janeen smiled. "I can understand that. Having your fiancée travel with another guy might be a little much."

"I know. The thing is, Jordan rarely spends time with me. He's busy with his horses, and he's not one who likes to go out at night. I'm surprised he agreed to go out tonight." She looked away, watching Mark and Jordan wind their way through the crowd. "I believe I mentioned to you earlier that I was never invited to parties and dances when I was growing up. Tonight is a revelation to me."

The men rejoined them.

Mark looked at Janeen. "I doubt they have places like this in Manhattan, do they?"

"Not quite," she replied, smiling.

Jordan looked around the table and said, "I hate to be the one to end a good evening, but I have to be up in a few hours to work with one of my horses."

Cindy looked stricken.

Mark glanced at her. "I can take the women home, if they'd like to stay."

Cindy and Janeen spoke at the same time.

"Oh, that would be great," and "Actually, I'm ready to leave, too."

Jordan looked at Mark. "Since Cindy wants to stay, would you mind taking her home later?"

Mark nodded. "Be glad to."

Cindy gave Jordan a quick look. "Are you sure you don't mind?"

"Not at all. Have fun, you two."

The crowd at the door was even thicker than when they'd arrived. He finally took Janeen's hand and threaded their way through the groups of laughing and talking people.

When they finally reached the door, people moved out of their way until they escaped into the gravel parking lot.

"Whew!" Janeen said, laughing as they walked to Jordan's truck. As soon as they'd walked outside, Jordan had quickly dropped her hand.

He opened the door for her. Once she was inside, he closed it and got in on the other side. She waited until they were in the truck and on the way back to his home before she said, "Cindy said you don't go out much. Thank you for taking me to see the dance hall."

"No problem. You could have stayed, you know."

"I was glad you brought up leaving. I'm more than ready to head back to your place."

"I hope I didn't step on your toes. As you could tell, I'm not used to dancing."

"You're a very good dancer. Someone taught you well."

He nodded. "Mom insisted we both learn."

They rode home in silence. Janeen felt content. She was touched that Jordan had gone along with tonight's plans.

Once they pulled up in front of the house, Jordan walked around and opened her door, helping her down from the truck.

"Despite the fact that you really don't like me, you've been a very good host, Jordan," she said, turning toward the house.

Once inside the kitchen, he replied, "I don't dislike you. I'm just not comfortable with new people."

"You're a modern-day hermit."

He smiled. "Probably." He paused, ran his fingers through his hair and said, "The thing is—" He stopped. "I don't know how to say this."

"If you're afraid of hurting my feelings, don't be. I'm tough. I can take it."

"Okay," he said slowly. "Here goes." He cleared his throat. "Having you here is driving me crazy. I keep thinking about you no matter how hard I try to get you out of my mind. I don't want to be attracted to you. I'm going to marry Cindy."

Janeen stared at him in disbelief. He couldn't be serious! Could he? She tried to think of something to say.

"The last thing I needed this evening was to see that you wear matching panties!"

Matching panties? What in the world was he talking about?

He muttered something under his breath and moved toward her. He pulled her to him and kissed her like a man would if he was dying of thirst and had just found a gushing fountain.

The kiss caught her off guard. He was shaking, and she started to pull away when he tightened his grip and deepened the kiss. His tongue teased her lips, and she sighed, opening her mouth in response.

Her knees shook, and she slid her arms around his neck to hang on. He shifted slightly, and she felt his thigh nudging her legs apart, his erection pressing against her.

The kiss seemed to go on forever, and Janeen was so turned on she was ready to drag him to the closest bed. When he finally loosened his hold and stepped back from her, she was almost too weak to stand.

What was happening here? They were panting. She stared at him in confusion. The man she thought she knew had stepped so far out of character that she couldn't think of anything to say.

Finally, Jordan ran his hand through his hair, causing it to stand up in tufts. "I'm sorry," he said, his voice rough. "That was a stupid thing to do, and I have no excuse to offer you. It's just that I've been waking up at night to discover that I've been dreaming you were there in bed with me and I was—" He stopped abruptly.

She was stunned. This was the man who had made it clear that he wanted no part of her being there...and he'd been dreaming about her?

"I, uh, I'll see you in the morning," she said and hurried out of the room.

Jordan shook his head in total disgust with his behavior. He hadn't been so turned on by a woman since he'd been in college, but that was no excuse to attack her as soon as they got home. How could he have lost control that way? He was a grown man, not some teenager with raging hormones.

He'd wanted her so badly that he'd thrown away his sense of honor and decency. She made him feel vulnerable for the first time in years, and he hated feeling that way.

He reminded himself that Janeen would be leaving his ranch soon. She couldn't stay here. Tonight he'd discovered that he was much too susceptible to her.

He'd call Jake in the morning and tell him he couldn't keep her here. He shook his head in disgust. All he needed was for Jake to ask him why. He wondered if "she's driving me crazy" was enough of a reason. Otherwise, he'd be forced to face the fact that he was in lust with a woman who was not his fiancée.

Eight

Coffee.

Janeen's caffeine-deprived body finally nudged her awake. She could smell the sirenlike scent somewhere nearby. She turned over and reached for— Janeen woke up with a start. She'd been dreaming. Something about Jordan morphing into an irresistible lover who—

She sat up and dropped her face in her hands, resting them against her bent knees. Jordan had kissed her. Worse than that, she had kissed him back. She'd been so turned on she'd had a miserable time later trying to fall asleep. She'd been sensitive to the touch of her nightshirt—even the sheets—and she'd spent most of the night tossing and turning.

Because of Jordan.

How was she going to be able to face the man ever again?

She glanced at her watch and immediately felt better. It was almost eight o'clock. Jordan had gotten up hours ago and was already working with his horses. There was a good chance she wouldn't see him all day. At least she had some time to pull herself together before she had to face him.

Coffee was the key. Janeen quickly dressed and went across the hall to the bathroom. She forced herself to look in the mirror and winced. She looked like she'd been partying too hard. She hadn't bothered to remove her makeup before going to bed, and now she looked like a raccoon.

She reached for a washcloth and scrubbed her face. Next, she brushed her hair into a topknot at the crown of her head. It was the best she could do until she consumed several cups of coffee. She wasn't ready to face the day just yet.

Janeen headed for the kitchen and spotted the coffeepot as she walked into the room. She found a large mug and poured the steaming liquid into it. With a groan of pleasure, she sipped the coffee and slowly turned to lean against the counter, only to choke and sputter when she saw Jordan seated at the table on the other side of the room.

"Sorry," he said quietly. "I guess I should have let you know I was here."

Still coughing, Janeen managed to get out the words, "You think?"

"Why don't you sit down and enjoy your coffee?"

She could think of several pithy responses, none of which could be uttered to her host at the moment. Instead, she walked over and sat down across from him.

"I thought you'd be outside working," she muttered, lifting her mug to her mouth, admittedly hiding behind the act of drinking.

"I have been. I decided to get a cup of coffee and thought I'd wait to speak to you."

Great. All she needed to start the day.

"An apology for my behavior last night is the least I can do. I certainly don't want you to think it could happen again. There was no excuse, and I don't plan to make any. I thought you'd want to know that you're safe around me."

She studied him as she drank her coffee. He hadn't looked

away during his speech, and he couldn't hide his discomfort. He'd obviously been running his fingers through his hair. He didn't look as if he'd gotten much more sleep than she had.

Finally, she knew she needed to say something in response. "I understand you acted out of character last night," she finally replied.

He looked surprised by her remark.

She went on. "I know you're engaged. I've done my best not to cause you any concern while I've been here. Given the circumstances, I believe the best thing for me to do is to leave."

"I can't lie to you and pretend that you don't have a strong effect on me. Under the circumstances…" He paused as though running out of words.

"I know. We're both uncomfortable with this situation, and there's no reason to prolong it. Thank you for your apology and your honesty. I can't pretend that I wasn't an active participant last night. I'm embarrassed by my response to you. I believe we both agree I should leave today."

He straightened without taking his eyes off her. "Maybe it's for the best," he finally said.

"Yes."

Jordan nodded and stood. "If I don't see you before you leave, take care of yourself."

She smiled. "Always."

He picked up his hat and put it on, pulling the brim down, leaving his eyes shadowed. She watched him walk out the door.

How would she feel if he wasn't engaged? She didn't know. She'd seen so many sides of him that she wasn't sure who he really was. Not that it mattered at this point.

Janeen poured herself another cup of coffee and went back to her room to call Lindsey.

Jordan strode toward the barn, disgusted with himself. He needed to call Jake and explain to him what a lowlife he was—engaged to one woman and kissing another one.

He hadn't slept much the night before, thinking about the whole situation. He had asked Cindy to marry him. She accepted. She was the kind of woman he needed in his life. It irritated him that he could be so attracted to another woman when he was already committed. Was this some kind of test of his integrity?

If so, he wasn't looking too good in that department.

He reached the barn and headed to his office/tack room. He needed to call the feed store and place an order. The phone rang as soon as he stepped inside his office.

He picked up the receiver. "This is Jordan," he said.

"Hi," Cindy replied. "I know you're busy, but I really need to talk to you. Could you come over?"

He glanced at his watch. "Okay. I'll get over there as soon as I can. I've got a few things to take care of first."

"That'll be fine. I'll be here whenever you can make it," she said and hung up.

He knew something was up. The phrase "I really need to talk to you" had always had an ominous ring to him. People talked to each other all the time, so why did they need to make an appointment to discuss something?

He wondered what infraction he had committed to cause the phone call. Was she upset that he'd left her with Mark rather than wait to take her himself? Or was it because he'd taken Janeen home? What made a great deal of sense to him last night might be open to another interpretation.

He'd done great all these years without a woman in his life. Now there were two of them. He was at a complete and total loss when it came to understanding women.

Lindsey answered on the third ring.

"How are things at your place?" Janeen asked.

"Much better. In fact, I was thinking about calling you today to see if you're ready to return to Houston."

"I'm all for it. It won't take me long to pack."

"Great. I'll see you shortly."

Janeen closed her cell phone and stared at the wall. There was one thing she wanted to do before she left there. She hurried into the kitchen.

The stallion was looking her way when she stepped out on the porch. When she walked toward his pen, he greeted her with a whinny and took careful steps as he made his way toward her.

He'd never done that before! The carrots must be working their magic on him. She hoped he wouldn't be disappointed when she held out an apple. He stopped and looked at her. She continued to talk to him in a soothing voice, holding the apple rather than placing it on the ground.

His ears went forward as he continued to move cautiously toward her. She stayed perfectly still when he was close enough to arch his neck and delicately take the apple from her, immediately chomping into it.

Moving her hand slowly, she gently touched his jaw. He flinched, and she waited until he relaxed a little before she lightly stroked his head. "You are such a dear. I'm going to miss you."

Jordan walked out of the barn and spotted Janeen actually touching the stallion. What did she think she was doing? He strode toward her. The stallion jerked his head up and immediately began to dance away from the fence.

"That was a really stupid thing to do, unless you don't care about keeping that hand."

Janeen took a deep breath before she turned to face him. "I don't think he's afraid of me. A man or men must have abused him. He and I are becoming friends."

"Hardly."

She was used to this Jordan. "Lindsey will be here soon." She held out her hand. "Thank you for your hospitality. Seeing this place has given me a new appreciation for the hard work ranchers do."

He took her hand, and she could have sworn electricity

sparked when their hands touched. They immediately stepped back from each other.

"I'm headed over to Cindy's," he said after a pause. "I don't know when I'll be back." He certainly needed time to make amends with Cindy, even if she didn't know what had happened last night.

"Tell her goodbye for me. I enjoyed getting to know her."

Janeen watched Jordan walk to his truck, his long legs covering the ground quickly. His well-worn jeans clung to him, emphasizing the muscles in his hips and legs. She watched him as he got into his truck. She really hadn't needed any reminders of how well-built he was, not after last night when she'd been plastered against him.

Their kiss would haunt her for a long time. She hadn't wanted to see him as an attractive male, given the current circumstances. The tension between them had been steadily escalating since she arrived, and she supposed their kiss was the inevitable outcome of the sparks flying between them.

Janeen went back inside to pack and wait for Lindsey.

Jordan didn't see Cindy when he first drove up and figured she was out in one of the pastures with her horses. He walked down the hill and soon spotted her. He smiled. She loved her horses.

When she spotted him, she strode toward the fence and vaulted over it. She wore her hair up, but because it was considerably shorter than before, tendrils of hair fell around her face.

"Mornin'," she said. "Thanks for coming over. I wanted some privacy for our talk, and I thought over here would be better."

"Actually, Janeen is leaving today, but I didn't mind coming here."

Cindy looked surprised. "She never said a thing about leaving yesterday or even last night."

He shrugged without looking away from her. "Her stay was only temporary. I didn't expect her to be there long."

She motioned for him to follow her over to one of the large

live oak trees that dotted the area. She'd thrown a couple of saddle blankets on the ground.

"I hope you had fun last night," he said, settling onto one of them. "Hope you didn't mind my having Mark bring you home."

She flushed. Maybe she was angry, after all.

"Okay," she said after taking a deep breath. "Here's the thing. Remember when you asked me to marry you? We looked at all the reasons why a marriage would work. We have a great deal in common and we like and respect each other."

Uh-oh. His heart began to pound in his chest. Did she already know what had happened after he got home last night? Had Janeen called her? No, of course not. Cindy had been surprised to hear that Janeen was leaving, which was a good indication that they hadn't spoken this morning.

"All right, what's this all about? Are you upset because I left early last night?"

She smiled. "Not in the least. I enjoyed last night immensely. I got to see some nightlife and be a part of it."

"That's good. I'm glad you had fun." He scratched his ear. "So what's the problem here?"

"When was the last time you kissed me, Jordan?"

"Huh? What does that have to do with anything?"

"You don't remember, do you?"

"Of course I do! I kiss you all the time." What the hell was going on with Cindy?

"Actually, Jordan, you don't. Oh, you kiss my cheek once in a while, but that's it."

"Well, then," he said, feeling more and more frustrated, "I guess you're going to have to take me out and shoot me for dereliction of duty or something."

Maybe he should go back home and start his day over. It certainly wasn't going well so far.

She gave him a half smile. "That's my point. I don't want you to think of our relationship as a duty."

"Okay," he finally said. "I thought our getting married was

something we both wanted. Have I missed something here? Have you changed your mind?"

Cindy twirled a piece of grass in her fingers. She didn't answer him right away, which definitely made him nervous. When she did, her answer surprised him.

"I remember when you were in college and dating one of your classmates. You were so happy with her. I figured you'd be married by the time you graduated. Only you weren't. Instead, you withdrew from everyone around you."

He removed his hat and shoved his hand through his hair. "That happened a long time ago, Cindy. What does that have to do with anything?"

"I think you asked me to marry you because you thought I'd be safe."

Oh, boy. Now it was his motives being questioned. Why was it women always wanted to talk about feelings and stuff? Why couldn't they just accept things, like he did?

"I hope you can explain that remark because I don't have a clue what you're talking about. Safe? Safe from what?"

"From getting hurt again. I think that eventually you decided you wanted a wife and family. You looked around and there I was. You knew I wouldn't hurt you. You knew me, you understood me, and I was available."

He didn't like this conversation. Not at all. He controlled the urge to get up and walk away. Finally, he asked, "What kind of remark is that? It's ridiculous, that's what it is. You're talking like I picked you out of a herd or something."

She clasped her hands around her raised knee and looked off into the distance. In a reflective tone, Cindy said, "I knew when you asked me that you weren't in love with me. At the time, that didn't matter to me. I was caught off guard because I never expected anyone to ask me to marry him."

"That's nonsense, Cindy. You have a lot to offer. Don't belittle yourself."

She looked at him a long time. Her intent gaze made him

uncomfortable. What did she want him to say? What was she looking for from him?

Finally, she lightly touched his jaw with her fingers. "You're a very nice man, Jordan. You're honest and up-front. I have no doubt you'd be a good husband…just not for me."

He stared at her, feeling the shock of her words run through him. "You're telling me you're breaking our engagement?"

"I'm telling you that we should never have gotten engaged in the first place."

He could feel his anger building. "When did you happen to decide all of this? You seemed just fine last night."

"I believe the thought has always hovered in the back of my mind, knowing that I had agreed to marry you for all the wrong reasons. I finally faced the fact last night."

He should have known. He'd been an idiot to think she wouldn't be hurt by his actions, but was that any reason to end the engagement? He wanted to shake her, but of course he didn't. Instead, he shook his head. "Look, I'm sorry I left the dance early last night. Looking back, I can see that it was really a dumb thing to do. We can work through this. I know we can. We can set a date today, now, for the wedding. I'll do my best not to be so inconsiderate again. If I am, give me a good kick in the rear, okay?"

She shook her head. "I'm so sorry, Jordan. I didn't realize how difficult this was going to be." She turned and looked at him. "The reason I'm calling off the engagement isn't about you and me. It has to do with Mark."

"Mark! You want to break up with me because of Mark?"

"I want to end our engagement because I realized that I had decided to settle for a quiet, peaceful, steady life, and I know I would have that with you."

"Settle, huh?"

"Just like you settled with me. No fireworks, no grand passion and no vulnerability."

"You've decided all of this because of something Mark said or did last night?"

She shook her head. "It's a little more complicated than that." She looked away from him, and he saw her face turn red. "Would it surprise you to learn that I have had a crush on Mark since we went to school together?"

Jordan kept getting hit with one surprise after the other. He frowned. "Yeah, it would. You never let on that you had a thing for him."

She almost whispered the words. "Last night was the first time he truly noticed me after all these years."

"So you decided to marry me as a last resort, is that it?"

She made a face at him. "Just as I was a last resort when you couldn't marry the woman you were in love with in college."

He closed his eyes and shook his head. "I can't believe we're having this conversation."

"I didn't think there was any reason to tell you how I felt about him. I thought I'd eventually get over him, and to be honest, I never thought it would matter."

"I see."

"After Mark took me home, we sat and talked for hours. He opened up to me in ways I would never have imagined. Of course I didn't tell him how I felt about him. It would have been wrong since I was engaged to you. He'd said something earlier in the evening that struck a chord with me. He mentioned that I should start following the rodeo circuit. He said he or Jack would always be around for protection if I needed it. I had to face the fact that I really wanted to do something like that…start traveling…see the country. I wasn't ready to get married. It wouldn't be fair to either one of us. That's when I knew we needed to talk."

"If you're looking for my blessing, I'm not sure I can give it. Mark's the kind of guy who will never settle down. So if you expect him to marry you—"

"Not at all. What he suggested would be a new and different life. Maybe I'll hate it, but I won't know that until I try it. I'm not ready to jump into a relationship with Mark, but I would like to see what might happen if we spend more time together."

Jordan had trouble taking all of this in. Finally, he said, "I don't want to see you hurt."

"I know. I appreciate your concern more than I can possibly say. I'm sorry if I've hurt you by doing this."

He had to get out of there. He didn't want her feeling sorry for him! "I'm sure I'll survive," he said, coming to his feet. "I need to get back."

She also stood and surprised him by kissing him. It was pleasant and familiar, and it was nothing like his kiss with Janeen.

Cindy had proven her point, even without knowing it.

Nine

Jordan drove home on autopilot, stunned by Cindy's decision to break up with him. He never saw it coming. He thought she was happy with him. He thought they would have made a good couple. Instead, she was willing to risk getting her heart broken by spending more time with Mark. Even if he'd known about her feelings for Mark, he wouldn't have seen him as a threat to their relationship. Their pasts had nothing to do with today. Or so he'd thought.

When he got out of his truck, he glanced at the activity in the pens. His help knew their jobs and were following today's schedule just fine.

Without going over to where they were working, he turned and went into the house, which was silent. He checked the bedroom where Janeen had stayed and wasn't surprised to see she was gone. He seemed to have a real knack for running off women. Two in one day had to have set some kind of record, though.

Kissing Janeen last night was unpardonable, and he knew it. Especially when he'd had trouble stopping. He would have much preferred to have carried her into his room and made love to her all night. Not exactly the thoughts and feelings of a fiancé. Cindy was probably right about his reasons for getting married...and she wasn't even aware of what had happened with Janeen the night before.

He couldn't understand himself. He was acting totally out of character. What was she talking about that he didn't want to feel vulnerable? As far as that went, he'd like to know of one person who actually enjoyed being vulnerable.

He made himself a sandwich, washed it down with warmed-over coffee and left the house. He'd find something to do to keep busy. He'd do just fine without a woman in his life.

"You're really being quiet," Lindsey said on their way to Houston that afternoon. "Are you okay?"

"Of course. I've enjoyed being in Texas."

"Good. Maybe you'll come back to visit soon."

Janeen smiled. "Probably."

"We'll go to Galveston tomorrow and enjoy the beach. I promised the children they would be able to go now that they're no longer contagious."

"Sounds good," Janeen replied.

She couldn't decide whether or not to tell Lindsey about what happened between her and Jordan. It really hadn't amounted to much. A kiss. That's all. So why was she making such a big deal about it? Probably because she had no business kissing Cindy's fiancé and she was embarrassed and ashamed of her behavior.

The chemistry between them had been so unexpected that she'd been caught off guard. Because he'd been so distant with her she'd been convinced he disliked her. She knew he disliked the fact that she'd been shoved off on him. He'd made no effort to hide his reluctance to have her living at his ranch.

He'd been dreaming about her? How could that possibly be true?

Of course she'd started having her own dreams about him—shockingly erotic dreams, at that—and she'd been convinced she did not like him in the least. His kiss had stirred up something in her she'd never experienced with anyone else. How crazy was that?

She had to put him out of her mind. She'd be flying home next weekend. She would return to her old routine and get on with her life. She would consider her time with Jordan as an aberration of some kind and chalk it up to experience.

Lindsey had warned her that the Crenshaw men had a way about them. Janeen could second that.

She wondered if Cindy would send her a wedding invitation.

The phone rang once the next morning and was answered immediately. "This is Jake."

"Jake? Hi. This is Jordan." The latter sat in his office with his boots resting on his desk, drinking coffee.

"Hey, buddy," Jake replied, sounding cheerful. "How are things going for you now that your company has left? Still ready to shoot me for getting you involved?"

If he only knew. "Of course not. She wasn't any trouble." He paused and stared out the window. "I was wondering if I could come over and talk to you about a few things that are on my mind. Do you have time this morning?"

"Jordan, I always have time for you. That's a given. Come on over."

"Okay."

"In fact," Jake went on to say, "I've got to hunt down a cougar—at least that's what I think it is—that's been bothering my cattle. Care to join me?"

"Sounds good. See you."

Jordan hung up. Well, he was committed. He had no intention of discussing Janeen with anyone. Whatever it was about her that had kept him on edge was gone. He had plenty of other things to run past Jake.

Forty-five minutes later, Jordan stopped his truck in front of Jake's barn and got out. He found Jake inside tightening the cinches on each saddled horse they would take.

Jake glanced up. "It's been a while. Glad you could visit. I'll enjoy the company."

Jordan nodded.

Once in the saddle, Jake headed southwest to the rugged country that was part of his ranch. Jordan knew it would take them close to an hour to reach the area Jake wanted to search.

"So what's up?" Jake said finally.

Jordan cleared his throat. He wanted to give him the facts. "I guess the reason I'm here is to tell you that Cindy broke our engagement."

A couple of beats of silence passed before Jake said, "I wasn't expecting to hear that!" He leaned forward in his saddle and looked closely at Jordan. "What in the world happened? I hope to hell it wasn't because Janeen was staying at your place because if it was, I really screwed up."

"Actually, she and Janeen hit it off right away. Janeen encouraged Cindy to cut her hair and buy some fancy clothes. I never figured Cindy to be one of those women who worried about her looks." He shrugged. "I guess you never know about women."

Jake laughed. "So you're just now learning that, are you?" He sobered. "Did she give you any reason?"

"She said that she wanted to travel and see something of the country. I think she has more confidence in herself with her new look. She pointed out that I asked her to marry me because I felt safe with her and not because I actually loved her. Oh, and she mentioned she was interested in Mark Shepard and wanted to follow the rodeo circuit with him."

"Holy sh— Cindy? I would never have believed it. I thought she was content to stay here."

"Surprised me, I can tell you."

"*Do* you love her?"

Jordan gave the question some thought. In a reflective voice, he finally said, "I've spent most of the past twenty-four hours asking myself that. Maybe I don't know what love is because I thought we got along fine."

"Hmm. This came out of the blue for you, didn't it?"

"Yeah." He shook his head. "To say my luck with women is bad is an understatement. I keep falling for women who reject me."

"So what are you going to do?"

"Not a lot I can do. She said she's had a crush on Mark for years but he'd never noticed her. I guess once Janeen got Cindy all duded up, Mark finally noticed her in a big way. I don't think Mark will marry anybody and settle down, but Cindy said she didn't care. I have a hunch the constant traveling will get old for her after a while but only time will tell."

"If she changes her mind, do you think you'll take her back?"

Jordan slowly shook his head. "Frankly, even if she comes back home, I don't think she'd ever *want* me back."

"So Janeen *was* at least partly responsible for the breakup, wasn't she?"

"Not really. If this is the way Cindy feels, I'm glad I found out before we got married."

"Good point."

They fell into a companiable silence while they continued their ride. Jordan felt a little better after discussing the matter with Jake, although he was uncomfortable with the fact that he hadn't mentioned the kiss that seemed to loom front and center in his mind. Had Cindy sensed something between him and Janeen? Not that Janeen had done anything to make anyone think she cared a thing about him. He'd been the one playing the jealous fool with her from day one.

Funny. He'd never been jealous of Cindy. So what did that tell him? That he was lower than a snake, no doubt. Maybe

Cindy had been right. Maybe they had decided to get married for all the wrong reasons. His ego had definitely been stepped on, but considering his strong reaction to Janeen, he deserved whatever Cindy did.

As the ground grew rougher, the men traveled single file down into a ravine. There was no more conversation as they hunted for the big cat.

Janeen and Lindsey were packing for their beach excursion when the phone rang.

Lindsey went to the phone. "This is probably Jared," she said as she picked up the phone. "Hello?"

"Lindsey?"

"Yes."

"Hi. Uh, this is Jordan."

"Oh, hi, Jordan. I'm sorry I didn't get to thank you for allowing Janeen to stay with you."

"Yeah, okay. I was wondering, is she still with you, or has she already gone back to New York?"

Lindsey smiled. "Actually, she's right here. Hold on, I'll let you talk to her."

Lindsey handed the phone to Janeen, her eyebrows lifted.

Janeen took the phone, her heart suddenly racing. She took a deep breath and said, "Hello, Jordan."

"Hi. I, uh, never asked you when you're going back to New York."

"I'm here for another week. Why?"

"Well, that is, I, uh…"

She waited. She knew that Jordan was a man of few words, but the few words he was saying now left her in the dark.

He cleared his throat. "I didn't want you to leave on bad terms."

"I didn't."

"Okay, well, I thought that, maybe, I could visit you in New York sometime."

Janeen took the phone away from her ear and stared at it as

though the receiver had something to do with his out-of-left-field remark.

Finally, she said, "Jordan? What's this all about? And please don't expect me to believe that you're missing me."

He laughed. She wasn't certain she'd ever heard him laugh before. "The truth is that I'm attracted to you. We both know that by now. I'd like to pursue the relationship if you're interested."

What a creep. How could he do this to Cindy? In her coolest tones, she said, "Somehow, I don't believe that Cindy would appreciate our pursuing a 'relationship.'"

He was quiet, and she hoped he got her message. Then he said, "Well, actually, Cindy broke the engagement the morning after we were out dining and dancing. It seems that Mark is her one true love, and I doubt she cares what I do anymore."

Janeen sank into the nearest chair. "Oh, Jordan. I'm so sorry."

"I can't say that I'm jumping with joy, myself. But the thing is, I've had to face the fact that I reacted too strongly to you."

"As I recall, you made it clear what you thought of me."

"That's my point. I showed more emotion while you were here than I have with anyone. I tried to convince myself that it was because I didn't like you. As it happens, I was fooling myself. You got under my skin more than anybody I know. I've had to ask myself why."

"And did you come up with an answer?"

"Yeah. I'm an idiot for not understanding the reason for my behavior sooner."

"I see." She supposed she did. Sort of. The man had her going in so many directions that she was spinning.

"I'll understand if you never want to see me again, believe me."

She sighed. "It's a little tough to have a long-distance relationship, you know."

"I know. I thought if I went to New York and saw you there, I'd better understand who you are and where you're coming from. You've managed to find out a lot about me and I know very little about you."

"Even if I thought I knew you—which I don't, by the way—the very last thing I would have thought you would do is want to come to New York."

He didn't say anything. Janeen looked up and spotted Lindsey unabashedly listening to her end of the conversation. Janeen blushed. This was really awkward.

Oh, what the heck. She rattled off her phone number and her address. "We can try this, but don't expect miracles. As you so ably pointed out, we have little to nothing in common."

"I'll keep in touch. Thanks," he said and hung up.

She slowly put down the phone and stared into space.

Lindsey said, "What an interesting one-sided conversation that was. Was there more going on when you stayed at his place that I don't know about?"

Janeen stood. "Not really. His call was quite a shock."

"What was that about Cindy?"

"She broke their engagement."

"Because of you?" Lindsey asked in surprise.

"Oh, I don't think so. I watched them together, and I never got the impression they were madly in love with each other. In fact, they acted like a long-married couple, pretty much doing their own thing.

"I suspected that she was settling for marriage with Jordan. Neither of them showed much enthusiasm about setting a date. When I saw her with this rodeo guy, Mark, I saw sparks flying everywhere."

"Then Jordan's fortunate to be out of it."

"Yes."

"Do you think he's on the rebound? That *that's* why he called you?"

Janeen shrugged. "Who knows? He's a complete mystery to me. I couldn't believe he mentioned visiting me in New York. How bizarre is that?"

Lindsey picked up the last load to put in her SUV. "You could do worse, you know."

Janeen followed her out to the car and helped load supplies. "Oh, can't you just see me making my home on a ranch in Texas?"

"Depends on whether you're in love with the guy...or not."

Janeen sighed. "I didn't really think I even liked him."

"What changed your mind?"

Janeen straightened and said, "Oh, I don't know," she replied vaguely. "Maybe he's like a fungus and grows on you."

Lindsey shook her head. "You do what you want. But if I were you, I'd definitely encourage his interest. No telling where this all might end."

"In bed, that's where!"

They both laughed, and Lindsey went back inside to round up her kids.

Ten

The morning after she returned home, Janeen called her dad on his private line at his office.

As soon as he answered, she said, "I'm b-a-a-ack" in a singsong type of voice.

"Good for you, gorgeous. Did you enjoy Texas?"

"Well. Yes and no. I enjoyed the part where I stayed with Lindsey. However, I stayed with one of her in-laws for almost a week and he was less than thrilled to have me at his place."

"He?" Of course he would pick up on that! "Tell me more," he said. She could tell he was smiling.

"He has a horse ranch. He raises quarter horses, trains and boards and supplies stud service."

"And you didn't enjoy that? I'm surprised. You love horses."

"That hasn't changed. It's just that Jordan is— Well, he's— I don't know how to describe him. He doesn't talk much, and when he does, he's brusque. He has a great deal of patience with his horses. It's being around people that he finds difficult."

Her dad laughed. "So you didn't like him, I take it."

She paused before saying, "I wouldn't say that, exactly."

"Aha! Care to tell me more?"

"Well, I thought I'd come up to see you guys this weekend, but I need to know if Mom is still irritated with me. Wait. Never mind. Mom is always irritated with me."

"Your mother loves you and you know it."

"My mother smothers me and you know it."

"She's doing better since you left home, I think."

"If only I wasn't an only child."

"I understand. You need to understand that after two miscarriages your mother was so happy to have you. She wanted your life to be perfect."

"That's the problem, Dad. She wants my life to be the way she wants it to be, regardless of how I feel. So if I come, will you promise not to tell her until I walk in? Act surprised to see me."

She heard the amusement in his voice. "She isn't that bad."

"Really? You know that if she has any warning at all that I'm coming up, she'll plan something—a dinner, a dance, a cocktail party—to trot out the men she considers to be eligible for me to marry. It's so embarrassing."

"I know."

"It's not that I don't love her, it's that she never listens to a thing I say. She just bulldozes her way into my life and is determined to plan who I marry, where we'll live, how many children we'll have, where they'll go to school, what clubs they'll join. Shall I go on?"

"Try to understand her point of view."

"Why? She doesn't bother to listen, much less understand, my point of view. I don't know how you've lived with her for all these years."

"That's easy. I love her. I know how vulnerable she is where you're concerned. You could cut her a little slack, you know."

Janeen rubbed her forehead where a headache was forming. "I know."

"So let her have the fun of having a party for you. We haven't seen you since Christmas, and we miss you."

Janeen sighed. "All right. You've managed to lay on the guilt trip thick enough to make me cave."

"That's my girl."

"Your thirty-two-year-old 'girl,' by the way. I really am all grown up, you know."

"There are times when I have to wonder. You're behaving like a child at the moment."

She gave that some thought. "I guess you're right. I'll be up this weekend, and I promise I will be on my best behavior, okay?"

"I'll believe that when I see it. What you've never understood is that you and your mother are very much alike—you both think you're always right and never wrong, you're both stubborn and determined to get your own way—yet in spite of all that, I somehow manage to love you both."

They both laughed. "So you're saying that if I have a child, I'll treat him or her the same way? What a horrible thought!"

"Maybe you should plan to have more than one."

"Maybe I should find a husband first."

"If you don't want your mother looking for one for you, I'd suggest you find one yourself. What about the man you brought up to see us last fall?"

"I found out he's a creep."

"Shall I beat him up for you?"

"No. So maybe my taste in men isn't all that great."

"Never tell your mother that you think such a thing. She'll be having every eligible man she meets fill out an extensive questionnaire."

Janeen choked and started laughing. "And she would, too! I really miss you, Dad. I'm looking forward to seeing you."

"Same here…and your mother will be thrilled. Bye now."

She shook her head as she hung up the phone.

She could have done much worse for a mother—one with

addictions, one who ignored her, one who belittled her. Janeen made up her mind that she would follow her dad's advice and stop acting like a child.

Janeen's phone rang that night. It was probably her mother telling her about the party she was planning for the weekend.

"Hello?"

"Uh—hi."

"Jordan?"

"Yeah. I was sitting out here on the porch, watching the moon come up, and for some reason I thought of you."

She dropped into a chair. "That's nice." Thank goodness she sounded calm, despite the fact she was shaking with nerves. What was that about?

"Was your flight okay?"

"Yes."

"Any delays?"

"No."

"Well. Guess that's good."

Silence fell between them. Grasping for something to say, Janeen asked, "So how's the black stallion?"

"He's okay."

"Are you giving him carrots?"

"Um, no. He gets fed like the rest of them."

"Oh." After a moment, she said, "Are you going to sell him?"

"I wouldn't do that to some prospective buyer."

"I mean, once you get him over being scared of people… men."

"Probably."

She couldn't think of anything more to say.

Finally, he said, "I guess I should let you go. You're probably busy."

"Thank you for calling. It's good to hear from you." *Even when you don't talk much.*

"Take care of yourself," he said gruffly and hung up.

Janeen slowly put the phone down. Jordan Crenshaw had actually called her. For some reason, she hadn't expected him to call. What did they have to say to each other? She pictured him sitting on his porch in one of his rocking chairs, looking at the night sky. Mentioning it was the most romantic thing he'd ever done where she was concerned.

She went into her bedroom and got ready for bed. When she finally fell asleep, she had a smile on her face.

Her parents met her at the door Saturday morning. She gave them both a big hug.

Her mother looked very patrician with her hair in a chignon and her face carefully made up. Her dress was emerald green, the color of her eyes. Janeen hugged her. "It's good to see you, Mom."

Her mother blushed and nervously touched her hair. "You know how much I love having you here."

Her dad enveloped her in a bear hug. "You're looking good. Got a nice tan while you were visiting Texas."

"We spent a couple of days on Galveston Island before I came home."

Her mother tucked Janeen's hand over her arm and said, "We're having a little dinner party tonight, just for you."

"Really?" she asked, giving her dad a quick glance. "That's sweet of you."

"We're having all your favorite food." Her mother guided her to the back of the house and motioned for her to sit on one of the lounge chairs on the terrace.

Janeen smiled. "Thank you. I hope you didn't go to too much trouble."

Her mother laughed. "You know how I enjoy having people over."

"Yes, Mom. I do."

The weekend went surprisingly well, and by the time Janeen was driving back to the city, she thought about her mom, the perfect hostess. There were new faces there—all eligible men, of course—as well as several of her friends, whom she hadn't seen in a long while.

She needed to come up more often. She loved her mom, at least in small doses. Her mother would have made an excellent military general. She got a great deal done even while she exhausted those around her.

She wondered what Jordan would think of her mother. That was one meeting she hoped to see someday. Jordan was like no one her mother had ever met. Janeen grinned. Maybe they would go visit Texas someday.

Once Janeen was in bed, her thoughts returned to Jordan, revisiting the memory of the kiss they'd shared…and the way he looked in jeans…and the way he walked…sauntered, actually…and his eyes. Oh, my…and the expression in his eyes when he finally let go of her that night in his kitchen.

He hadn't said anything about calling her again. What would be the point? Even though he'd mentioned coming to New York, she couldn't picture him here.

She wondered how he was doing. The horse, of course.

Whenever Janeen thought of the ranch house where she'd stayed, she smiled at the thought of what her mother would say if she saw it. It had been obvious that most of the money available had been spent on the horse barns and buildings. His house appeared to have been an afterthought.

The men she'd visited with while at her mother's party were attractive and attentive, and she could barely keep herself from yawning in their faces during their conversations. She'd decided that if she met someone with whom she thought she could form a relationship, she intended to allow it to happen. So why did her dreams continue to be peopled with tall, lean and handsome men wearing cowboy hats?

She really needed to get Jordan out of her system.

He called her the following weekend.

"Hi. This is Jordan," he said in his deep, drawling voice. "How was your week?"

"All right. I visited my parents last weekend in Connecticut."

"Sounds like fun," he said and she almost laughed. Actually, she had enjoyed herself.

"Everything okay with you?" she asked.

"Yep. I wanted to let you know that I gave the stallion a carrot this morning. I didn't actually give it to him, you understand. I placed it inside his pen, and he finally went over to check it out once I left." After a pause, he added, "I think he misses you."

She laughed. "Somehow I doubt it."

There was another long pause. Finally, Jordan said, "So." She waited because she had no idea what to say. "I was wondering if you have made any plans for tonight?"

Puzzled, she replied, "Not really, no. Why do you ask?"

"I was wondering if you would have dinner with me."

"You're here?" she blurted out, immediately embarrassed by the question. Of course he was here! "I mean, yes, I'd like that."

"I'm not sure about the local customs," he said, as though he was visiting a foreign country. She could hear the smile in his voice. "What time do people generally eat around here?"

"I don't know about most people, but I generally eat around seven-thirty."

"I'll pick you up at seven, then."

"Or I could meet you somewhere. Save you from having to come here."

"I want to come there. I'll see you," he said, and hung up.

Janeen stood there listening to the dial tone buzz in her ear for a moment before she slowly replaced the receiver.

He was in New York. Jordan Crenshaw had actually come to New York. She was having trouble wrapping her mind around the idea.

Her next thought was highly original. *What am I going to wear?*

* * *

By the time a taxi pulled up in front of her apartment building, Janeen had changed clothes three times. She didn't want to be too formal, nor too casual. When Jordan stepped out of the cab, she was glad she'd gone with the dressy casual.

He wore a pair of western-cut slacks that made him look muscular and fit. She'd forgotten how the Texas sun had given him a deep tan as well as bleaching his hair. What was it about this man that kept throwing her off her stride? She was being ridiculous.

She grabbed her purse and left her apartment, making sure the locks were set. She met him on the stairs. "Hi," she said, smiling.

He glanced up and saw her. That smile of his flashed white in his dark face. "Hi, yourself." He waited for her to reach the step above his, putting them at eye level. "You are a sight for sore eyes," he said softly.

He was radiating heat…or was she the one who was suddenly overheated?

"It's good to see you, Jordan," she said, offering him her hand.

Instead of taking it, Jordan slipped his arms around her and softly kissed her.

Oh, my. She hadn't needed the reminder.

He released her and took her hand. "The cab is waiting."

Once outside, he opened the door, helped her inside and joined her in the backseat of the taxi.

He must have told the driver where they were eating because the driver seemed to know where to go.

Jordan turned in his seat to look at her and grinned. "My memories of you didn't do you justice. You're beautiful. Trite, I know, but true."

She gave her head a quick shake. "I'm sorry, but this is a trick, right? You're really Jordan's brother, aren't you? This is some kind of joke, I take it?"

He looked startled. "What would make you think that?"

She frowned. "Jordan never treated me this way. He could barely stand the sight of me."

Jordan shook his head. "I'm really Jordan. Do you want me to show you some ID?"

Oh, great. She hadn't been with him for more than a few minutes and had already accused him of lying to her. She was racking up points quickly if her goal was to get rid of him early.

She sighed. "Sorry. I didn't mean to—oh, you know—be rude."

"I thought I made it very clear to you before you left my place that I never disliked you. You were a distraction, that's all. I was engaged. My life was already planned, and then you came along and my plans sort of blew up in my face."

"I never meant for that to happen."

He reached for her hand and slipped his fingers through hers. "Oh, I'm well aware of that. There was nothing you did...except be you."

She looked down at their clasped hands, her fingers long and light, his much larger ones dark and scarred. Finally she looked up at him. "I don't know what to say. You've got me very confused."

He grinned. "Good. Then you know how I've been feeling. I finally decided I needed to do something about it, so here I am."

She could only look at him. His eyes were so blue and intent on her. He had already rubbed his thumb across her wrist and felt her pulse racing.

After several minutes of silence, he said, "I don't mean to come on too strong. I'm sorry if I've made you uncomfortable. How about we enjoy the evening together as old friends seeing each other again?"

She nodded. "Okay." Yeah, right. She'd never had this kind of reaction to an old friend.

The taxi stopped in front of a well-known restaurant. Jordan paid the driver and helped her out. Once on the sidewalk, she asked, "What made you pick this restaurant?"

He shrugged. "The concierge at my hotel suggested it. He made the reservation for us. Is there something wrong with it?"

She shook her head quickly. "Not at all. It's a very popular place, and it's difficult to get reservations. This will be my first time to eat here."

"That makes two of us," he said with a wink. He took her hand, and the doorman opened the door for them.

Once inside, Jordan gave his name to the maître d' and was immediately taken to their table in a little nook by a window that looked out on a garden.

"I'm impressed," she said with a smile.

Sober, he said, "So am I." He'd kept his gaze on her.

She blushed. Darn it, she could feel the heat. What was wrong with her?

They gave their drink order and looked at the menu. Janeen was so flustered that she had no idea what to order.

When the waiter returned with their drinks, Jordan asked for his recommendations. "Does any of that sound good to you?" Jordan asked her.

"Uh, actually, all of it sounds good. I'll have whatever you're having."

Jordan gave their order and once the waiter left leaned back in his chair and smiled. "Tell me what you've been doing since you left Texas."

"Not much, really. I've been checking to see if any of the museums have openings. So far I haven't found anything."

"Sorry to hear that," he replied blandly, his smile turning into a grin.

"Why do I get the impression that you're not all that sincere?"

He chuckled. "Look at it this way. If you aren't working, there's no reason you can't visit Texas again soon."

Once again he'd left her speechless.

"Tell me about your visit with your family."

"It went well, considering everything. I'm attempting to smooth the rough edges of my relationship with my mother. My dad said we don't get along because we're so much alike." She grinned. "He's probably right. I need to have more patience with her, I suppose."

He studied her with a smile. "You seem very different to me than you were in Texas."

She frowned. "Is that good or bad?"

"Neither. I suppose you're more comfortable in your own environment."

She felt far from comfortable, and it was due to her strong response to his presence. She searched for a change of subject. Finally, she said, "I didn't meet your parents while I was there. Do they live in Texas?"

"When they aren't traveling. Jake's dad and my dad are brothers. They and their wives are gone quite a lot. After being tied down to their ranches for years, they deserve to be able to take off whenever they want."

Their salads arrived, and while they were eating, Janeen suddenly had an idea.

"How long are you planning to stay?"

"Why? Wanting to get rid of me?" His relaxed expression softened his reply.

"Not at all. I was wondering if you'd like to go to Connecticut and see the horses we keep there, and maybe see some of the countryside."

"I'd like that."

She relaxed a little. "Good. We can drive up in the morning, spend the day and come back tomorrow night."

By the time their entrées arrived, Janeen had relaxed and enjoyed Jordan's company. They didn't have a future, but she could certainly enjoy the present.

They arrived back at her apartment later that evening, and Jordan asked, "Would you mind if I come up for a while?"

Since she wasn't ready for the evening to end, Janeen smiled. "I'd like that."

"Good," he said. He paid the driver and helped her out of the taxi.

On the way up the stairs, she said, "My apartment isn't very large, at least not according to Texas standards."

He paused and looked at her. "Are you nervous about my opinion of your place?"

Feeling foolish, she admitted, "A little."

They continued up the stairs. "I can't imagine why, after seeing my place."

They paused in front of her door, and she pulled out her keys.

"Are you sure you have enough locks to keep you safe?" he asked, showing his surprise.

She didn't look at him while she unlocked the door. "I live alone, and I want to feel secure."

"You must have found it strange that I never lock my doors."

Janeen opened the door and walked inside. "City life is considerably different from what you're used to." She closed the door behind him.

Actually the place was a nice size for a New York apartment, but as soon as Jordan stepped inside, the place seemed to shrink. She was suddenly reminded of the time when Lindsey had been staying with her and Jared had shown up at the door unannounced. It had been winter then, and he'd been dressed for the season. Even without the heavy coat that Jake had worn, Jordan had the same effect on the place.

He wandered over to the windows. "Don't I know it. I've never heard so much noise…horns honking, sirens going, people yelling. Does it ever get quiet here?"

"Not completely, no. There's always something going on."

He turned and looked at her. "My place must have seemed abnormal to you."

"I expected it since I'd stayed at Jake's place before I arrived at your ranch." She walked over and stood beside him, looking out at the street. "I'll admit it took a little getting used to. My parents' place is fairly quiet, so I can always escape when I feel the need to get away."

He turned toward her. He touched her cheek with the back of his hand. "I'd forgotten how beautiful you are," he said softly.

She blushed despite her best effort to accept the compliment. "Thank you."

He cupped her chin and leaned toward her, his mouth brushing against hers.

There was no reason now not to kiss him, except for the fact that she was in danger of falling for him. She pulled back slightly and with a bright smile said, "Would you like some coffee?" she asked, wishing she didn't sound quite so breathless.

He dropped his hands and shoved them into his pockets. He smiled ruefully. "Sure. I'm sorry for coming on so strong. I've been fighting the need to touch you all evening. Guess my self-control slipped a little."

She couldn't think of anything to say. "I'll, uh, I'll go make the, uh, the coffee. Be back in a minute." She went into the kitchen and set up the coffeemaker and then went into the bathroom. Her cheeks were flushed, her eyes bright and her hair seemed to be falling out of its sedate chignon. With a huff of frustration, she pulled it down, brushed it and pulled it away from her face into a ponytail.

Once the coffee was ready, Janeen set up a tray and carried it into the living room where Jordan was still standing.

"Oh! You should have found a seat," she said, hastily placing the tray on the coffee table before she dropped it. "I'm not a very good hostess to have forgotten to tell you."

"I've been looking at your photographs. There are a lot of you and Lindsey."

"Yes. We've been friends for years."

He turned. "I'm glad you decided to visit her."

The table was between the sofa and a chair. She took the chair and poured the coffee into cups.

He came over and sat across from her. "You don't need to be nervous around me," he said quietly, and she realized he'd seen her hands trembling. "I was hoping you would trust me enough not to take advantage of you. After all, we lived together for a few days, and outside of my behavior the last night you were there, you seemed to be comfortable around me."

"Mmm. I know. It's just that…the truth is that I haven't adjusted to the difference in you. You may remember lecturing me about everything I did when I was there. Now you're looking at me as though you want to, uh, you want to—"

"Make love to you?" he asked.

She swallowed. "I guess. I mean, you're like two completely different people."

He leaned back and relaxed against the sofa. "I can understand that. I came to see you in the hope that you would get to know me as I really am, which isn't the person you saw fighting my response to you." He took a sip of coffee. "I'm no longer fighting, as you've no doubt discovered."

"I never thought that you saw me as anything more than a nuisance."

"And now you know I don't consider you a nuisance at all."

She nodded and smiled. "I'm beginning to get that idea, yes."

"And it scares you."

"Well…not exactly…a little nervous, perhaps. I don't know what you expect from me."

He gave his head a quick shake. "Then I've done this all wrong. I told you I'm not very experienced dealing with women. I just knew I wanted to see you. So I came."

She touched his hand. "I'm glad."

They smiled at each other.

They continued to talk as time slipped by without either of them noticing. Janeen discovered that she enjoyed Jordan's wry sense of humor.

Finally, Jordan glanced at his watch and did a double take. "Is it really this late?" he asked. "Twelve-thirty?"

She glanced at her wall clock and chuckled. "It may be twelve-thirty in Texas but it's an hour later here."

He shook his head and pushed himself up from the sofa. "I didn't mean to spend the night!" His ears turned red. "I mean—"

She walked with him to the door. "I know what you meant. I'm not reading something into everything you say. I promise."

He paused at the door and said, "I can't remember an evening I've enjoyed more."

"The surprise of your visit, the wonderful meal and having you here have been very enjoyable for me as well. Thank you."

He stood there as though memorizing every feature of her face. After a moment, he slipped his hand around to the nape of her neck.

"Good night, Janeen."

This kiss wasn't tentative in the least.

Eleven

Janeen melted against him. The entire evening had been leading up to this moment as though they'd gone through hours of foreplay.

Jordan plucked out the band holding her hair and with a moan of pleasure ran his hands through the silky strands. He wanted nothing more than to pick her up and carry her to bed.

That thought caused him to step back from her.

Her lips were swollen and moist, and her glittering eyes were slumberous. He had trouble finding his voice while attempting to calm his breathing.

"If I don't leave right now," he drawled, "I'll be here all night."

Janeen smiled and trailed her fingers across his cheek. "Good night. I'll see you in the morning...at your hotel." She stepped back and opened the door.

He'd never been this turned on before. "I'm sorry to come across as a sex-starved jerk." He turned and walked out of her apartment.

She immediately opened the door and stuck her head out. "You want me to call you a taxi?"

In his condition? No way. "That's okay. I need to walk for a while. I'll flag one down later."

Janeen watched him go down the stairway until he disappeared from sight before she closed and locked her door.

She leaned against it, hoping her knees wouldn't give way.

She found a chair and sat, shaking her head. Speaking of love-starved behavior. She was all over him! She had to fight the impulse to drag him off to bed. Their heated kisses made it clear that she'd stepped over some kind of line in their relationship. Like it or not, she was hooked. His raw sensuality left her reeling.

She'd thought of taking him to her parents' place to show him the horses and to get him away from the city for a few hours. Lingering in his presence for much longer scared her. She didn't want to fall in love with him. She would only get hurt.

A long-term relationship between them would be a disaster. Her life was here on the East Coast, and she couldn't imagine Jordan living anywhere but his ranch with his horses and dogs.

So why was she tantalizing herself by spending another day with him? A great question. Unfortunately she couldn't come up with a logical answer because she had none. She was making decisions on an emotional level, something she rarely did where men were concerned.

Janeen went to bed and eventually fell asleep with dreams of kissing Jordan Crenshaw, but this time they were in bed with no sign of clothes.

Jordan's fast-paced walk took him to a more heavily trafficked area sometime later. By the time he settled in the backseat of a cab, he was perspiring. Once at the hotel, he spent a long time in the shower.

He'd spent the past ten days convincing himself that he needed to forget her. He'd already gotten himself in trouble once by falling for an East Coast woman. Why would he consider going through that again?

He didn't like the answer that came to mind. He had to face the fact that he was, in fact, falling for her. He'd actually hoped that seeing her in her own environment would be the wake-up call he needed to forget her and get on with his life. Or at least that was his reasoning when he'd found himself making reservations to fly to New York.

After his shower, he dried off and went to his bed, tossing the towel aside and crawling under the sheet. He lay awake for several hours wondering what he was doing in New York. The more he was around Janeen the more she tugged at him in so many ways. Her looks were great but it was her attitude to life that fascinated him. Despite his warnings, she'd insisted on making friends with the black stallion, and his dogs still looked for her around his place.

He needed to get on with his life, and he knew it. However, he was giving himself one more day to spend with her, a day that would have to last him a lifetime.

Janeen saw Jordan waiting beside the doorman of his hotel the next morning. She pulled over to let him get in, smiling at him. He looked sexy as hell in his jeans and western shirt. He wore his boots.

He strode over to her and slid into the car. Glancing around the interior of her fire-engine red sports car, he said, "Guess I should have known you'd be driving something like this. You don't see many of them in Texas. They're too low to the ground to be of practical use."

She checked traffic and pulled back into the flow. Janeen had dressed sensibly today. She'd wrapped a scarf around her hair, wore khaki jeans and an emerald-green shirt.

"I wouldn't dare venture into Texas in my little car. No one would see it from the cab of a pickup truck. I'd be flattened in no time."

She gave him a brief glance at the first red light. "I brought us some snacks in case you get hungry," she said.

"I ordered a substantial breakfast in my room. I'll admit I feel a little strange not having to do anything productive for a while." He looked her over. "You look cheerful this morning."

She gave him a quick grin. "It's a gorgeous day. Be thankful the humidity is lower than usual. Temperatures can be sweltering among the tall buildings. The sidewalks radiate heat from the sun as well. I'm looking forward to getting out of town again."

He pushed his seat back as far as it would go and stretched out his legs.

"Do you have enough room?" she asked, glancing sideways at him.

"I do now," he replied. "I feel like my rear's going to touch pavement if we hit a bump in the road."

Once out of the city, traffic thinned out a little and they made good time. Jordan asked questions about the areas they passed through, showing an interest that seemed sincere.

By the time they arrived at her parents' place, it was mid-morning.

Janeen pointed out their home but took the road that led to the stables. He studied her family home and its surroundings without comment. Once at the stables, they both got out. Jordan stretched as he got out and walked over to her. When he took her hand, the electric current between them intensified.

Once inside, she glanced at him with a smile. "You'll notice we don't have many horses. It's nothing like your place."

They paused and looked at each horse; all of them expected to be stroked and petted. She watched Jordan as he visited each one, rubbing their necks and murmuring to them. Of course they enjoyed another worshipping human in their life.

"I wouldn't expect you to," he murmured. He nodded toward the horses. "Looks like someone spoils them."

Janeen laughed. "Guilty as charged." She opened the bag

she'd stuck in her purse and pulled out carrots. "It's such a little thing to make them feel loved."

He grinned. "If I did that, I'd get so attached to mine I wouldn't be able to sell them."

"But you have some favorites. I've watched you."

"I guess you're right."

"Would you like to ride?"

He lifted his brow. "I didn't bring my saddle."

She laughed. "Oh, come on. You can manage on one of ours."

He walked to the entrance and looked at her home. Finally, he turned and said, "Do your parents know we're here?"

"Probably," she said absently, opening the stall and leading one of the mares out. "They'll see the car."

"Did you let them know you were bringing company?"

She stopped and looked at him. "No. It doesn't matter. They don't care who's with me."

Jordan helped her saddle the horses. She noticed that he didn't have any trouble riding "eastern-style."

They followed the horse trails as they wound in and around the trees, and Jordan enjoyed the ride.

They were following a meandering curve in the trail when another horseman approached them. The man stopped. "Janeen? What a surprise. Your mother didn't mention you would be here this weekend." His gaze went past her to Jordan.

"Jordan, I'd like you to meet a longtime neighbor of ours, Martin Krause. Marty, this is Jordan Crenshaw."

Jordan nudged his horse forward and shook hands. "Hello."

Martin shook his hand and leaned back in his saddle. "Do you live around here, Jordan?"

"No. I'm from Texas."

Martin's gaze darted to Janeen. "Texas. Didn't you tell me that you just returned from there?"

"Yes. My friend Lindsey married one of Jordan's cousins."

"Ah." Martin looked at them for a long moment. "How long will you be here?" He looked at Jordan but Janeen answered.

"We just drove up for the day. I thought I'd show Jordan where I grew up. He has a horse ranch."

Martin took in the jeans and western boots. "We do things a little differently here, as you can see."

Jordan nodded affably. "Yes. Janeen wanted me to see the contrast."

Janeen glanced at her watch. "We need to get back. It's almost time for lunch. Good to see you, Marty. Tell Louise hello for me."

"Of course." He turned to Jordan. "Enjoy your visit."

"I am. Nice meeting you."

Jordan waited until they were approaching the stables before he asked, "Is Louise his wife?"

"His sister. I'm actually closer to her than I am to him."

"Not of his choosing, I'm sure." He swung out of the saddle and reached up for her.

"We're friendly neighbors. There's nothing there."

"On your side. I saw that. The poor guy bristled when he saw me. I figured you'd allay his fears that I'm not any kind of competition."

"What an imagination you have." They led the horses back into the stable, unsaddled and wiped them down and gave them some oats before they drove to the house, parking in back by the multicar garage.

They entered through the side door of the building, which could easily be mistaken for a hotel because of its size, and walked along a hallway. "Hello," Janeen called. "Thought I'd let you know I'm here."

Janeen continued to lead him until they entered a garden-like room with glass on three sides. An older version of Janeen stood. "Hello, darling. If I'd known you were coming I would have planned—" Her voice got softer when she saw that her daughter wasn't alone.

"Mom, this is Jordan Crenshaw. I spoke to you about him."

Janeen's mother smiled and walked to where Jordan stood.

"I actually have a name besides Mom. I'm Susan White." She held out her hand.

Jordan kept himself from stiffening at the tone of her voice. She was saying all the right things, but there was a coolness in her manner of speaking. One that he'd heard before when he'd gone to Virginia. He wasn't "one of them." This time he wasn't bothered. He wasn't trying to make a good impression.

"You have a lovely home, Mrs. White."

"Please. Call me Susan. Janeen told us that she stayed on your ranch for a few days. It was bad timing when Lindsey's children came down with the chicken pox." She grinned. "Of course there's never a convenient time to get sick."

He smiled.

Susan turned to Janeen. "Have you two eaten?"

"We snacked."

"I'm certain you can eat some more. It's Grace's wonderful chicken salad today. Your father is playing golf, of course. He'll be home later this afternoon."

"We've been riding. Why don't we meet you in a few minutes after we've cleaned up?"

"Certainly. I'll just go tell Grace that you're here."

Susan smiled at Jordan again and left the room.

"Your mother is very nice," he said.

Janeen turned to him and crossed her arms. "What were you expecting…the dragon lady?"

Jordan smiled. "I had no expectations whatsoever."

"Somehow I doubt that. Come on and I'll show you where to wash up."

If Janeen's purpose was to make it clear to him how differently they had been reared, she'd succeeded. He'd known that as soon as he saw her for the first time.

She and Martin were typical products of this environment. One of the reasons—all right, the main reason—he'd come

East was to remind himself of who she was. What better way to accomplish that than by visiting her family home?

The chicken salad was every bit as good as its advertisement. The three of them chatted, keeping the subjects light. Susan surprised him with her interest in his ranch. She was full of questions about breeding and raising horses. After that she asked about the Crenshaw family in general.

"I met Lindsey's husband when Janeen brought them for a visit. He's related to you how?"

"He's my cousin. Our dads are brothers."

"You talk about your family with a great deal of affection."

Jordan nodded. "We're a close-knit group."

Susan looked at Janeen. "Nothing like your father's family. We seldom see them, and both sides prefer it that way."

She asked a few more questions, when Janeen finally said, "You know, Mom. You missed your calling. The government could use you as an interrogator."

Susan blushed. "I'm sorry, Jordan, I didn't realize how nosy I was being with all my questions. I've never been to Texas, and I'm fascinated by your life there."

He smiled. "I'm not offended. My life is nothing like yours."

"I'm sure you're right. However, I'm glad you had a chance to see and ride our horses. They're Ray's pride and joy."

"Do you ride?" he asked.

"I'm afraid not. Despite my best efforts to hide it, I'm afraid of them and, as Ray points out, they immediately sense that."

After lunch, Susan excused herself and left the room. As soon as she was gone, Janeen said, "I'm truly sorry that you had to go through such a grilling."

"I didn't mind." He didn't…because he'd expected something similar.

Janeen stood and held out her hand. "The truth of the matter is that Mother is intrigued by the fact that I've brought someone home to meet the family. This is only the second time I've done so."

"What happened to the first one? Did he disappear never to be seen again?"

She rolled her eyes. "I wish. No. That's when I discovered that he was much more impressed with my family's money than me."

"Ouch." He gazed at her. "You don't think I'll be the same?"

"Are you kidding me? The Crenshaws could buy and sell the entire state with their petty cash!"

"We have a lot of land. That doesn't necessarily equate to money."

"The truth of the matter is that I wanted you to see where I grew up, and I wanted you to meet my parents."

"Then your mission is almost accomplished." Jordan stood and took her offered hand.

Janeen turned and looked at him, her lips twitching. "Mother's been working industriously to find me a husband, and since I brought you here, she probably believes that I've chosen you."

They walked away from the dining area. Jordan chuckled. "Somehow I doubt that, although I have to admit she now knows everything about me except for my Social Security number!"

Twelve

"That's my mother, all right. I'm surprised she didn't ask about your dental health, how much you weigh and how you feel about children!"

He could feel himself turning red, and there wasn't a thing he could do about it.

She took pity on him and said, "Come on, I'll show you around this part of the country. That is, if you care to see it?"

He raised a brow. "And then what? A heart-to-heart chat with your father?"

Her smile was mischievous as she reached up and gave him a quick kiss. "Thank you for being such a good sport about all of this."

He looked at her. "You knew you'd get this kind of reaction, didn't you?"

"Let's just say I wasn't surprised. I also knew you could handle it."

As they walked to her car, Jordan looked around the carefully tended lawn and gardens. "It's a nice day. I wouldn't mind exploring."

Janeen realized that she was thoroughly enjoying keeping Jordan a little off balance and was impressed at how well he handled himself.

Once in the car, she turned to him. "You know something, Jordan? I like you."

He gave her a half smile. "You mean as long as we play Pin the Tail on the Donkey and I remain the donkey?"

"Not at all. I'm seeing a different side of you, the side you show when you're not doing your best to avoid me. Since I started out feeling you regretted agreeing to have me stay at your place, and now you actually seem to enjoy my company, I believe we've come a long way."

She started the car and drove back to the street.

"I'm enjoying having some time off, but basically I have very little life that doesn't revolve around my ranch."

Of course she knew that, which is why she was so surprised that he'd come to visit her. When she left his place, she'd been certain she would never see him again.

When they returned to her parents' home later in the day, her dad was there. She parked in front of the house behind her dad's BMW. "Oh, good. Dad's here. I bet Mother has filled his ears about you."

"You're certainly getting a great deal of pleasure out of all this."

She leaned across the console and placed her hand on his cheek. A long, lingering kiss followed. When she finally straightened, her lips were moist and a little swollen. Jordan fought the impulse to kiss her again and forget about her family, but he knew better.

As soon as they walked into the foyer, Ray White came strolling out of one of the front rooms. He grabbed Janeen and hugged her tightly. When he finally let her go, he kissed her on the cheek and said, "You certainly enjoy seeing your mother all atwitter." He turned to Jordan. "You may have already guessed that I'm Raymond White, Janeen's father." He held out his hand.

"Jordan Crenshaw. It's good to meet you." Jordan shook his hand.

Ray grinned. "At least I'm no longer outnumbered. Janeen and her mother tend to gang up on me when they get together." Her dad was sincerely friendly and yet his gaze was full of appraisal.

"I'll do my best to uphold the honor of males around here, Mr. White."

Her father laughed. "You'll do, my man, you'll certainly do. Oh, and by the way, call me Ray."

By the time Janeen announced that they needed to head back to Manhattan, Jordan had discovered that he really liked Ray White. He was funny and down-to-earth. Jordan had no idea how the man made his money, and he didn't particularly care. Susan had been reserved with him when they'd first arrived, but as the afternoon progressed, she had relaxed and seemed to be enjoying herself.

All in all, the day had gone all right, Jordan decided. He'd enjoyed seeing Janeen interact with her parents, and he realized that she didn't fit into the neat little stereotypical box into which he'd placed her when they first met. So why should he be concerned that he'd been stereotyped as soon as he admitted he was from Texas?

Jordan knew that if Janeen lived in Texas, he would spend as much time with her as she allowed. Despite his resolve, he knew his interest in her had only increased since he'd arrived in Manhattan. He had to face the fact that she didn't live in Texas and he would never live anywhere else.

Once back in Manhattan, Janeen said, "I'll drop you off at your hotel and—"

"No."

"No?" She looked startled. "Where do you want to go?"

"I intend to see you home."

"So chivalrous."

"Call it what you like. Just know that I'm not going to let you go home alone."

"Actually, I do that every day."

"Well, today, you're not."

Janeen said nothing more and drove to the underground parking garage that accommodated two of the apartment buildings. "Okay. I'm home," she said when she turned off the engine.

"You don't say. How long have you been living in a garage?"

She eyed him with a frown. "You know, Crenshaw, sometimes you can be a real pain in the patootie."

He smiled. "So I've been told."

She shrugged. "All right. You win." She got out of the car before he could reach her and strode to the elevators. They rode to street level and walked until they reached her building. He followed her inside and up the stairs. She was almost at the top of the stairs when he heard her gasp.

"Steve!" She sounded upset. "What in the world are you doing here?"

Jordan quietly followed her.

"Waiting for you. You seemed to have disappeared and I was determined—" He spotted Jordan. "Who the hell is he?"

"A friend."

"Well, tell your friend to take off. We need to talk. You seemed to have fallen off the face of the earth. I've been looking for you for weeks."

Jordan moved closer to Janeen and placed his hand on the small of her back. He looked at her with a silent question.

Janeen returned the look and answered by moving closer to him so that his hand slipped around her waist. "Steve, I told you several months ago that I wasn't going to see you anymore. I wish you would leave me alone."

Steve took his time studying first her and then Jordan, staring at Jordan's hand resting on her hip. "Look. I'm sorry if I offended you in some way. I don't know what I did but whatever it was I'm sorry. We were doing great. You even took me to meet your parents. I took you to meet mine. Don't throw what we have together away. I'm sure we can work it out."

Janeen went to her door and began to unlock it. "I've moved on with my life, Steve. I suggest you do the same."

Jordan caught a flash of fury on the man's face. Steve had taken a menacing step toward her when Jordan stepped in. "I don't believe we've met. I'm Jordan Crenshaw."

Jordan had about four inches in height on Steve whoever-he-was. The man stopped moving. Jordan heard the door open behind him. He glanced over his shoulder and looked at Janeen.

"Come on in, Jordan. I promised you coffee," she said.

Steve said, "You can't be serious, Janeen. Where did you find this yahoo, anyway?" He looked at Jordan as though he had a distinct odor and whatever he had must be contagious.

Jordan walked to the door. "I don't believe it's any of your business. Steve." He ushered Janeen inside and closed her door, which she quickly locked.

She leaned against the door with a sigh. "All right. Don't say it. If you hadn't been with me..." She allowed her voice to trail off.

He took her hand. "Hey, where's that coffee you promised me?"

She straightened. "Oh. If you really want some, I can make it."

Janeen hurried to the kitchen. Jordan looked out the window and watched to see if Steve had left. There was no sign of him. He turned and followed her to the kitchen and leaned against the doorjamb. "Should I be insulted that you took him to meet your parents?" he asked, grinning.

She turned and looked at him as though studying him. "I'll admit I'm not a very good judge of character, okay?"

"Ouch."

"Remember that I didn't like you at all when we met. I consider that a poor judge of character, don't you?" Her smile was mischievous.

He answered her smile. "That definitely soothes my hurt

feelings." A comfortable silence fell between them. "I bet he was everything you thought you wanted when you started dating."

She reached for coffee mugs. "I suppose."

"You only saw this side of him when you called off the relationship, right?"

She turned and put her hands on her hips. "How did you know?"

"Because I went through something similar several years ago. Only she was the one who ended things."

"You mean before Cindy?"

"Yes."

She placed the mugs filled with coffee on a tray, and he picked it up, carrying it to the living room.

Once seated, they reached for their cups. "Thank you for being here," she said. "I could have dealt with him, but to be honest, I'm tired of having to deal with Steve. He's used to getting his own way. He was one of the reasons I went to visit Lindsey, hoping he'd get the message that I didn't want to see him anymore. When I didn't hear from him once I got home, I naively thought he'd met someone else and would leave me alone."

"Have you ever considered that he may really love you and not your family money?"

"No. I knew him well enough by then to realize he wasn't— and isn't—all that interested in me as a person."

"What are you going to do about him?"

She shrugged. "I'm not sure. Even if I were to report him, he's not doing anything illegal."

"I think stalking is against the law. He seems to have an ugly temper if tonight was any indication."

They finished their coffee in silence. "How would you feel about me staying here tonight?" Jordan asked.

Startled by the request, Janeen said, "There's no need. Really. I'm safe here. The next time he bothers me I'll contact the police."

He shook his head. "That won't keep you safe. If he happens

to be watching for me to leave, I think we should let him think we were together tonight."

She smiled. "And what will happen when you decide to return to Texas?"

He frowned. "Good point." He studied her for a moment and then said in a light voice, "You could always come home with me, you know."

She chuckled. "I thought you'd had enough of my company at your place."

He shook his head. "I promise to give you more attention this time."

Janeen was more than a little tempted, but she knew better than to think her leaving would do more than postpone her dealing with Steve.

"Thank you, but I need to stay here."

He nodded and stood. "I guess I'll get on back to the hotel."

Janeen realized that she hated to see him go. She enjoyed being around this new Jordan very much. She reminded herself that any relationship would be too painful.

Without saying anything, she stood and walked toward him.

They moved to the door and Jordan said, "I really enjoyed today. We'll keep your parents guessing about my intentions."

She laughed, and he slid his arms around her, pulling her up tight against him. Only then did she realize that he was definitely turned on. She could feel herself blushing like a teenager.

"Your dad's a kick," he said. "It's obvious the two of you are close."

There was a gleam in Jordan's eyes that caused her pulse to race. She relaxed against him, her arms around his neck. Being so close to him was definitely a distraction. What had he just said? Oh, her father.

She nodded. "My dad and I have the same sense of humor. At times Mom doesn't know what to do with us."

She'd tried for a casual tone but her voice quivered a little. This man could turn her on faster than anyone she'd ever met.

"Well," he drawled, "good night."

Neither one of them moved. Finally, he softly kissed her on her forehead and then on her nose before he dropped his arms.

Jordan knew he had to get out of there now before he lost what little self-control he'd been hanging on to. The problem was that she wasn't cooperating. He was surprised when, instead of stepping back from him, her arms tightened around his neck. He knew he was sunk when she started kissing him— on his cheeks, his jaw and, finally, his mouth.

He lifted his head a few inches and whispered, "If we don't stop now, I'm not going to be able to stop."

Her answer was to continue to kiss him.

With a groan, he lifted her until she put her legs around his waist. He didn't want to take her there at the door like some kind of animal, but he wasn't sure if he could make it to a bed. Jordan strode down the short hallway and entered her bedroom. He sat on the side of the bed and looked at her.

"Are you sure, Janeen? Is this what you want?"

If she said no, he hoped he'd be able to walk away.

She leaned back slightly, which pushed her closer to his erection. He was afraid he was going to lose it right then and there. "We've been dancing around this since the first time you kissed me," she whispered. "I'm tired of fighting the attraction between us. Aren't you?"

He quickly unbuttoned her blouse. "You have no idea," he muttered thickly.

She reached for his belt buckle, and they raced to undress each other.

Jordan paused long enough to retrieve the condom in his wallet.

Once they were sprawled on her bed, she seemed to be touching him everywhere. Her hands slid from his chest downward. "Honey," he said with a gasp, "if you don't want all of this to end right here and now, please don't touch—"

Despite his warning she found and encircled him, delicately running her fingers along his length. Forget foreplay. Forget gentleness. He moved over her, and in one strong push entered her until he could go no farther. He closed his eyes and held his breath, afraid he'd embarrass himself.

"It's all right, Jordan," she said softly. "Just love me."

He let go and fell into a rapid rhythm that quickly brought his release. Before he could find the breath to apologize she climaxed as well, convulsing around him as she cried out his name.

He rolled to his side and, still within her, brought her with him.

They were both breathing hard, and he had only the strength to hold her close and breathe in the scent of her hair.

After a moment or two he began to touch her breasts, molding his hand around first one and then the other. He placed his mouth over one of them and gave a soft tug and she caught her breath.

Her eyes were still closed. She sighed and arched her back. He began to rock against her. Her eyes flew open. "Jordan?" she asked in a wondering tone.

He pulled her knee across him as he continued to kiss her, his tongue keeping time with his lazy thrusts. "Hmm?"

She sighed and began meeting his movements with hers.

She felt so good, better than his wildest fantasies of her. She was warm and passionate and he couldn't get enough of her.

Eventually his slow rhythm quickened, and Janeen came apart in his arms, pushing him over the edge.

They fell asleep in a tangle of limbs.

Jordan woke suddenly, disoriented until he realized that Janeen was curled up next to him. He eased out of bed and went into the bathroom. He looked at his watch and saw that it was a little after six.

He returned to bed and cuddled her to him, pulling the covers over them. He'd made love to Janeen White. Was that what he'd planned when he came up here to see her?

Not necessarily, but he was sure the thought had been there somewhere, since he'd wanted to make love to her since the first day he saw her. He'd known then that she didn't belong in Texas. Nothing they shared now could change the basic fact that they had no future together.

He realized as he lay there holding her close that at some time—and he wasn't certain when—the woman had wrapped her hand around his heart and taken possession of it.

He'd been miserable since she left the ranch. At the time he'd attributed his feelings to the fact that Cindy had called off their engagement. How long had it taken him to face how much he missed Janeen?

This weekend would be a moment when they'd stepped out of time together and had forgotten everything else but being with each other. His missing her would never go away, he knew, but he'd have memories of being with her, making love to her and facing the fact that he'd fallen in love with her.

Janeen slowly opened her eyes to face sunlight peeking through the blinds. She lay on her side with Jordan curled around her, his hand cupped over her breast.

Wow. If she hadn't found him next to her this morning, she would have believed that last night was a dream. Janeen vaguely remembered kissing him goodbye and not wanting him to leave. She blushed when she recalled how she had thrown herself at him.

She had never done that with any man before last night. However, after spending the weekend with him, she'd known that her feelings for him were too deep to be ignored.

Was she sorry?

No, but his opinion of her behavior would probably have an adverse effect on his view of her. She cringed with embarrassment. What could she say to him this morning? An apology for her behavior would be a good start, she supposed. Then again, he certainly hadn't wasted any time getting her into bed.

She smiled...remembering.

When she attempted to slip out of bed, Jordan pulled her back to him. She turned her head and saw that he was awake.

"Mornin'," he said, smiling. "This is a very nice way to start a new day." He leaned over her, kissing her with unabashed passion, bringing her heart rate up to a new level. The kiss quickly escalated until they were both panting, his erection pushing against her thigh.

Janeen shifted until he eased down between her legs and gently entered her.

How quickly she had become addicted to his touch. She scattered kisses across his muscled chest and heard him draw a long breath when her tongue touched his nipples.

There was no urgency this morning as they explored and kissed each other until he shifted and lifted her hips slightly. She gasped at the new angle and clutched him when he rapidly increased his thrusts until they both exploded with mind-blowing pleasure.

Jordan buried his face in her hair. She fought for breath, and he moved to his side, still holding her tightly against him.

When she could finally speak, she traced his eyebrows with her finger. "So here's my question." She paused.

He opened his eyes and smiled at her. "What is it?"

"Do you respect me this morning?"

He looked startled and burst out laughing. He squeezed her to him. "Yes, ma'am, I sure do respect you and would like nothing better than to continue to respect you for as long as possible." He nuzzled her ear.

"Another question?"

"Okay."

"Why didn't I see this side of you when I was staying on your ranch?"

He released her and rolled onto his back. He stared at the ceiling for a while and she wondered if he intended to answer her, when he said, "Other than the fact I planned to marry someone else, I didn't want to take advantage of you."

She nodded thoughtfully. "Good point."

He leaned up on his elbow and studied her. "It's a little late for me not to take advantage, though." He kissed her nose.

"I was thinking that I'd taken advantage of you."

"I don't think you need to worry about that," he whispered and gathered her into his arms.

By the time they got out of bed, it was late morning. After breakfast he helped her with the dishes and then said with a hint of regret, "I need to go back home today."

Her heart stilled and then began to race. Trying for a light tone, she said with a strained smile, "I see. Once you've had your way with me, you're ready to head out."

"Not necessarily." He cupped her face with his hands and stared into her eyes. She'd never seen him so serious. He seemed to be looking into her soul.

"Meaning what, exactly?" she asked, a slight quiver in her voice.

"You can go back home with me, if you choose."

Thirteen

Janeen stared at him in shock. Had he said what she thought she'd heard? When she didn't say anything in response—words had deserted her—Jordan smiled ruefully, stepped back from her and dropped his hands.

"Guess that's my answer, isn't it?" He nodded. "Take care of yourself," he said, straightening. He left the kitchen and headed to the door.

Coming out of her stupor, Janeen chased after him. "Wait!"

He turned and looked at her patiently.

"You—you can't—can't say something like that and then waltz right out of here!"

"What more is there to say?"

She wrapped her arms around her waist. "Are you asking me to visit? To move? What?"

He shrugged. "Whatever you want to do, darlin'."

She fought down the panic that threatened to overwhelm her. "Well, I can't just—" She waved her hand. "You know, just decide today that I'll go to Texas."

"I understand." He turned to go.

"I can't just—" She ran out of words.

He looked back at her. "I'll make it easier for you, okay? You live here in the East. This is your home. Texas is, maybe, a great place to visit but you'd never want to live there. I get that." He unlocked the door and opened it. "Think of me once in a while, okay?"

She watched him go down the stairs without looking back. Once she heard the entrance door open, she closed hers and absently locked it. Only then did she realize that tears were running down her cheeks.

What had just happened here?

Janeen had absolutely no idea. Jordan had shown up on Saturday and was leaving today—Monday. They'd spent this time together. What did that mean to him?

What did it mean to her?

The man had kept her off balance since he'd first arrived. He hadn't asked anything of her, had gone along with whatever she suggested. He'd been receptive to their visit to her parents' home. None of that would have been what she'd expected of him.

She sank to the sofa. How could he make love to her the way he had and then calmly walk away? Janeen again wrapped her arms around her middle and rocked in total confusion. The man made her crazy. Of course he had to go home. She could understand that. What she didn't understand was why he'd come in the first place.

Most importantly—why did he suggest she go home with him? Could he be asking her to marry him?

Several days later she called Lindsey. When she answered, Janeen asked, "Do you have time to chat?"

Lindsey laughed. "Of course. I'm sitting here enjoying another cup of coffee. How are you?"

"I wish I knew. That's why I decided to call. Maybe you can help me figure out what's going on."

"I hope so. Is the job search discouraging?"

"No, actually, the Met just called me back part-time. This isn't about my job. It's my personal life."

"Your personal life? I thought you told me you don't have a personal life. Have you finally fallen for one of your mom's offerings?"

"No. This is about Jordan."

A long silence ensued.

Finally, Lindsey said, "Are you talking about Jordan Crenshaw?"

"The very one."

"Okay," she said slowly. "What's up with you and Jordan?"

"Uh, well, funny you should phrase it just that way. I ended up going to bed with him."

"You did what?!" Lindsey said, her voice rising. "When? How? Where?"

"The how is the easiest to answer. We kissed and then—"

"Very funny. Since you would have told me if you'd come to Texas, this must mean that Jordan was in New York?"

"Yes, over the past weekend."

"Unbelievable."

"I know. I have no idea why he came. He took me to dinner Saturday night. I took him to see my folks on Sunday. He spent the night here with me and the next morning announced that he needed to fly back that day."

"Did he say anything that would let you know his reasoning for being there?"

"The implication was he came to see me."

"What did your parents think about him?"

"They appeared to like him. I had a weird feeling that Mom wanted me to get measured for a wedding gown immediately. You know how she is."

"When he left, did he say he'd call, come back, that he loved you—something?"

"What he said is what I'm stewing about. He suggested I go home with him."

"Oh. My. God. He proposed?!"

"That's what is so confusing. He didn't propose. He didn't say whether he was inviting me to come visit him or move to Texas or whether he was suggesting that I marry him. The man is driving me crazy! Oh, Lindsey, I saw a new side to him that is irresistible. I think I'm in big trouble."

Janeen could tell that Lindsey was smiling when she said, "Those Crenshaw men are truly awesome, you've got to admit."

"I'm not certain he intended to make love to me, which is embarrassing to admit."

"Oh. So you tied him up and had your way with him? The poor man."

"No! Of course not. It's just that as soon as I saw him I could scarcely think about anything else but making love with him, like some love-starved teenager. I thought if I took him to see my parents, we wouldn't spend as much time alone. Unfortunately, the longer I was around him—watching him visit with Mom and Dad, showing him around the area, that sort of thing—the more drawn to him I became.

"I managed to control myself until that night when we were here in my apartment and he was leaving."

"Don't stop now," Lindsey said, chuckling. "Don't keep me in suspense. What happened then?"

"I couldn't let him leave," Janeen replied with a groan. "I'd been in this state of arousal all day and when I kissed him goodbye I discovered that he was just as aroused as I was." She paused, remembering. "Oh, Lindsey, he was so wonderful."

"Wipe the drool from the phone. Yes, I know about the Crenshaw men, therefore, that's a given. What did you say when he invited you back to Texas?"

"Say? I was too stunned to say anything. I mean, my life is here. I can't just jump on a plane and live happily ever after in Texas."

"I did."

"Well, your situation was different. I recall that you thought Jared had been forced to marry you. You actually left Texas because of it."

"Okay, okay. What I mean is after that."

"All right. I'll buy that, except for one important omission on Jordan's part."

"What?"

"He didn't ask me to marry him. Actually two omissions. He didn't bother telling me he was in love with me. He didn't mention his feelings at all." She almost wailed that last part.

"Did you?"

"Well...not really."

"Did you tell him you loved him?"

"Of course not. I'm too confused to know how I feel about any of this."

"I'd say the two of you parted with the same feelings of uncertainty, don't you think?"

Janeen thought back over the weekend. "I have no idea how he felt when he left," she finally said. "As far as I knew, I wouldn't see him again...until he said I could go home with him. That's what's so confusing. I don't know what to think!"

"Do you think he was serious or maybe just teasing you?"

Janeen didn't answer.

"Hello? You still there?"

Finally, Janeen said softly, "I don't think he was teasing. I remember the look on his face. He looked very serious."

"Well, then. Seems to me that the ball is in your court. Once you decide how you feel about him, maybe you can let him know."

"This is my home. I work here. I'm close to my parents, which I'll admit wouldn't have mattered a few years ago. How can I leave?"

"Guess you have to decide who or what you love most. Then your decision will be made."

Janeen rubbed her forehead, the headache she'd had when

she woke up throbbed more painfully. "What should I do? Call him and demand that he make an honest woman out of me?!"

Lindsey laughed. "Who knows? That might be a start to a serious conversation between the two of you." She paused before saying, "You have no idea how he feels about you, right?"

"Right."

"Then ask him, why don't you? Wouldn't that be better than the limbo you're in?"

"Maybe. Maybe not. Limbo seems safer at the moment. I'll have to think about it."

"Or…"

"What?"

"If you don't want to call him to discuss it, maybe you should come back for another visit."

"I'm not sure that—"

"Don't be silly. Come back and see how he responds to you. I know! Jake and Ashley are having a big Fourth of July barbecue. Why don't you plan to visit? Wouldn't that give you a reason for being here that has nothing to do with Jordan and his enigmatic invitation?"

Janeen swallowed hard. "He won't think I'm chasing him?"

"He might think you're interested in him. That's a plus, you know."

"I'll think about the idea."

"You do that."

"Thanks for listening, Lindsey."

"That's what friends are for."

Several days passed with Janeen going back and forth about what she should do. She waited for Jordan to call her. Finally, she decided to be bold and call him.

The phone rang several times before he answered and he sounded out of breath. As soon as he said hello, she asked, "Did I catch you at a bad time?"

"Janeen?"

"The one and only."

"Hey, gal, how are you?"

At least he sounded happy to hear from her, which went a long way toward reassuring her that he wasn't irritated that she called.

"I'm doing all right. And you?"

She could hear voices in the background. "Do you have company?"

"Oh. No, that's just some of my crew. We're, uh, just keeping ourselves busy. You know how it is."

"I won't keep you. I just wanted you to know that I've been thinking about you. Is there a chance you might be coming this way anytime soon?"

He covered the phone and said to someone, "Yeah, that's it. Just put it over there." He turned back to the phone. "Sorry about that. It's a little hectic. As much as I'd love to see you again, I'm going to be tied up here at the ranch for a while. The invitation for you to visit is still open, you know."

"Oh. That's what you meant…that I should come for a visit."

"What do you mean?"

She cleared her throat. "Oh. You know." She waved her hand as though he could see her. "You mentioned my going back home with you when you were here."

"I believe I did. You sounded as if you wouldn't consider it."

"I guess I was wondering whether you meant that I should visit or move there."

There was a long silence. "Well, the thing is, I've been turned down a couple of times so far when I suggested marriage. I figure I'm going to be a bachelor all my life. If you lived in Texas, maybe we could get together once in a while. If you're interested."

Well, there it was. Marriage was the last thing on his mind. Why not? He'd never indicated how he felt about her. Did he think she regularly fell into bed with someone?

Obviously, he did.

"Like you said, there's half a country between us," she finally said. "Guess we'll have one of those long-distance relationships."

"Is that what you want?"

She sighed. "Jordan. You've got me really confused. At this point I have no idea what I want."

"Well, let me know when you decide, okay? Look, I've got to go. I'll call you." He hung up.

"You do that," she muttered, replacing the receiver.

At least the phone call had accomplished one thing. She now knew he wasn't interested in marrying her. She'd needed to know that. She just wished the news didn't hurt quite so much.

It was Friday once again and Janeen knew she didn't want to stay in Manhattan. She threw some of her clothes in a bag and went to visit her parents.

She and her mother were sitting in the sunroom having coffee Saturday morning when Susan asked, "Have you talked to your cowboy friend?"

"Yes. Earlier this week."

"Will he be visiting again soon?"

"I doubt it."

"He seemed quite likable."

"Yes, he is. He's quite busy. He spends long hours working with his horses. I doubt he has much spare time. We're friends, that's all."

Her mother arched her brows. "Really? That surprises me."

Now what was she talking about? "Why?"

"Oh, there was something about the way he looked at you when you were unaware, a certain intensity, that made me think he was quite interested in you. He was very open to your father about his financial situation as well, as though he might be looking for approval from us."

"You obviously misread him." Her father had grilled him about his prospects? Wasn't that just great! She'd at least learned one thing: she would not be bringing any more male acquaintances home to meet her doting parents!

"Perhaps," her mother replied with a knowing look. "Do you have a date for the dinner-dance tonight at the Club?"

"No. I thought I'd go with you and Dad and visit with friends. I want to start back early in the morning, so I won't stay too late."

Another week went by. She thought about Lindsey's idea. She could visit over the Fourth without looking like she couldn't stay away from him. Couldn't she? If she happened to run into Jordan while she was in Texas, fine, but mostly she needed to spend some time with Lindsey. It was obvious that Jordan didn't love her. She really wouldn't care if she didn't see him at all. At least she spent a great deal of time convincing herself she wouldn't.

Fourteen

"**I**'m so glad you decided to come down for the Fourth of July," Lindsey said, unloading Janeen's bag from the back of the SUV.

Janeen smiled. "Me, too. When do you plan to go to Jake and Ashley's place?"

"I thought we'd drive over tomorrow and help Ashley get everything ready. Just a typical Crenshaw get-together with plenty of food for everyone. Jared said he'd meet us there. He's going to fly into Austin and rent a car."

"Doesn't his traveling get to you?"

"Sometimes. When one of the children gets sick or when I'm under the weather, I'd love to have him here to help or take over, but I manage." She winked. "And the homecomings make up for his absences."

"At least you share the same home. I can't see a relationship working when we live in two different parts of the country."

The conversation ended as soon as they entered the house,

where the children eagerly greeted their aunt Janeen. It was only later when the kids were asleep that Lindsey and Janeen sat at the kitchen bar and sipped wine.

"I've been thinking about what you said earlier," Lindsey began.

Janeen laughed. "Since I've been talking nonstop since I arrived, perhaps you can narrow down the subject matter for me."

"How much convincing would it take to get you to move to Texas?"

Janeen didn't answer right away. "A very good question," she finally said. "I've been asking myself if I would go that far to be closer to Jordan. I really don't think so."

"What if Jordan asked?"

Janeen quickly shook her head. "He won't. We've already discussed the idea."

"But what if?"

"I have no answers. I start back full-time at the museum in the middle of the month. My routine is getting back to normal. There's no reason to give that up."

"What if he told you he loved you?"

"Yeah, right. Remember, Jordan's a man of few words. I can't imagine him saying those particular words."

"Be bold. Be brave. Tell him how you feel about him."

"I don't think so, but thanks for the suggestion, old friend. At least I'm no longer bothered by Steve. Jordan's presence that night must have been what Steve needed to finally get the message that I was no longer interested in him."

"Well, you'll see Jordan at Jake's house."

"That's right. I need to practice my acting skills—you know, friendly but not too friendly, interested but not too interested, that sort of thing."

"Or you could throw yourself into his arms exclaiming how you don't think you can live without him."

Janeen turned her wineglass up and drained it before she said wryly, "I suppose that's an option." She stood. "In the meantime, I'm going to bed."

Lindsey hugged her. "I'm so glad to have you here."

Lindsey and Janeen arrived about midmorning from Houston. Janeen was amazed to see how well organized the women were as they prepared enough food to feed such a large group of people. She supposed they'd had enough practice.

That afternoon, Janeen looked up from scrubbing vegetables to discover that Jake had walked in with Jordan right behind him.

"Look who's here, everyone," Jake said, nodding toward Jordan. "Haven't seen him in a coon's age."

Jordan grinned and said hello until his gaze fell upon Janeen. With a heated glance he said, "Well, hello, there, sweetheart. I know I've never seen you before because you're definitely on the unforgettable list."

Janeen froze. Of all the greetings she'd expected from Jordan, not remembering her hadn't been anywhere on the list. Talk about ego deflating. She attempted to smile.

"Now, c'mon, Jack. You don't have to hit on every single woman you meet," Jake said.

Jack laughed. "Oh, so now I'm supposed to hit on every married woman?"

Jake shook his head and said to Janeen, "I'm sure you've guessed that this ladies' man is Jack Crenshaw, bull rider extraordinaire. No doubt Jordan mentioned him to you."

All at once Janeen felt lighter than air. She held out her hand. "Hi, Jack. I'm glad to finally meet you. Jordan told me a great deal about you."

"Don't believe a word of it," he replied, taking her hand and raising it to his mouth. He brushed his lips across her knuckles. "How do you happen to know my recluse of a brother?"

Ashley spoke up. "Oh, she stayed with Jordan for a few days last month."

Jack straightened. He gave Janeen a hard look. "Oh? Are you the reason Jordan broke off his engagement to Cindy?"

Before Janeen could say anything, Jake spoke up. "No, she isn't, you idiot. Your habit of speaking whatever thought crosses your mind keeps your foot firmly in your mouth, Jack. Jordan surely told you that Cindy broke the engagement to be with Mark."

Jack turned and looked at him. "No kidding? He never told me what happened." He glanced at Janeen. "I guess I put two and two together and got eight. Sorry about that."

"Speaking of Cindy," Jake went on to say, "have you seen much of her since you've been on the circuit?"

"A few times. She's amazing, and she's already winning some prizes." He scratched his head. "I asked about Jordan when we first met up, and she was the one who told me they were no longer engaged. Knowing Jordan, I figured he was the one who backed out." He turned back to Janeen. "So, pretty lady, where are you from?"

"I live in New York...Manhattan."

Jack laughed. "Now I *know* Jordan wouldn't be interested in anyone from back East."

Ashley said, "Tell me something, Jack. Have you ever heard of the words *tact* and *diplomacy?*"

"It's all right, Ashley," Janeen said, smiling. "I heard early on about Jordan's opinion of any woman from the eastern seaboard."

In an attempt to change the subject, Jake asked, "Have you seen Jordan since you got back into town, Jack?"

"I talked to him on the phone this morning. The folks are home and planning a big spread tonight for the two of us. We'll get caught up on all our news then."

Lindsey asked, "Have you met anyone special in your travels, Jack?"

He draped his arm around her. "Honey. I've met many of them."

"Not ready to pick one?"

He grinned. "That'll be the day. I'm a certified and con-firmed bachelor. I have no intention of settling down."

"C'mon, Jack," Jake said, filling two cups with coffee. "Let's go into my office before you're lynched by these three ladies."

Jack made a courtly bow. "Please accept my apologies if I have offended anyone. It was never my intention." He picked up his cup and followed Jake out of the room.

Janeen looked at Lindsey. "*That* was Jordan's brother?" she asked in disbelief. "They couldn't be more different."

Ashley said, "I'll admit that Jack is a little obnoxious—"

Lindsey and Janeen said at the same time, "A *little* obnoxious!"

Ashley shrugged. "He takes a little getting used to but he grows on you."

"Like a fungus," Janeen muttered, and the three of them began to chuckle and then laughter took over.

From Jake's office, they heard him holler, "There's way too much levity going on in the kitchen for anyone to be working."

His comment only made them laugh harder.

"Have y'all been drinking?" he continued to holler.

"What a great idea!" Ashley said, wiping tears from her eyes. She went over to a well-stocked wine rack and pulled out one of the bottles. "After that, we could all use a little something to calm our nerves."

Everyone was up early the next morning. Jake had started cooking the meat in the smoker the night before, and the aroma made Janeen's mouth water. Several women arrived early with salads, large bowls of different vegetables, pies, cakes and cobblers.

"Do you really expect everyone to be able to eat all of that?" Janeen asked, following Ashley to one of the long tables that had been covered by a tablecloth. They placed their bowls on the table.

Ashley said, "By the time everyone arrives you'll think a horde of locusts came through, devouring everything in sight."

Jared arrived about an hour later. Lindsey hadn't heard him and was busy when he walked into the kitchen, her back to the door. He held his finger to his lips for Ashley and Janeen, leaned over and kissed her on the nape of her neck.

She jumped and whirled around. "Jared!" She threw her arms around him and kissed him thoroughly, to the point that Janeen wondered if maybe she and Ashley should give them some privacy. She glanced at Ashley, who winked at her.

Eventually, the kiss concluded and Lindsey said, "I could have cut my finger off!"

"Nah. I waited until the knife was on the cutting board before I touched you."

"Have you seen the kids?"

"Nope. Guess I'd better go look for them." He grinned at the three women. "See you later."

As soon as he was out of the room, Janeen started fanning herself. "Whew. I think the temperature went up several degrees in here."

Lindsey grinned. "Ashley has the oven on," she innocently pointed out.

"Oh, I'm sure that's why," Janeen replied tongue-in-cheek. "I should have thought of that."

People started showing up soon after Jared arrived. Jake and Jared set up several tables outside while the women brought the rest of the food out to the table.

Janeen recognized many of them from the barbecue she'd attended last month, the one where she had first met Jordan. So far, he hadn't arrived. Who knew? He might skip the whole thing.

She spotted the man she now knew was Jack Crenshaw helping a young woman out of his truck by grabbing her around the waist and whirling her around in his arms before putting her on her feet. She wore a great deal of makeup, had long blond hair and her jeans and tank top must have been sewn on. Janeen could definitely see why Jack would choose her.

Janeen turned around and went back inside. "Anything I can do to help?"

Ashley said, "You've done enough, believe me. Go get some food and visit with everyone." She looked around the room. "Lindsey seems to have disappeared." She grinned. "I bet we couldn't find Jared right at the moment, either. She'll show up soon enough. Go. Enjoy yourself."

Janeen wandered outside, feeling a little lost. Everyone seemed to have so much to say to each other. She didn't want to interrupt any of the conversations.

She thought of Lindsey and how happy she was. Janeen wondered if she would ever find someone she'd love in the same way. Thinking that she might as well get in line for some food, Janeen walked toward the laden tables. She was caught off guard when someone touched her shoulder.

"Janeen?"

She would recognize that voice anywhere. She turned and saw Jordan. He was staring at her as though she was an apparition suddenly manifesting itself in front of him.

Okay. She'd prepared herself for this. He looked even better than her memories. With his broad chest in a red shirt, jeans molding his narrow waist and long, muscular legs, he was the sexiest man there. She reminded herself not to follow her first impulse, which was to throw herself at him and fiercely kiss him.

Instead, she smiled and said, "Hello, Jordan. It's good to see you."

Understatement.

He looked a little dazed. "Why didn't you call to let me know you'd be in Texas? This is wonderful," he said, his gaze checking her out from her head to her toes. When their eyes met, Janeen could practically feel the steam coming off both of them. Of all the people she'd met in her life, why was it this one who affected her so strongly?

He touched her chin with his thumb. "I take it you're here with Jared and Lindsey?"

"That's right."

He glanced around. "Why don't we get some food?" He took her elbow and guided her over to the food line, placing her in front of him once they got there. He stood considerably closer than necessary to her. She could feel the heat of his body along her back. She jumped when he placed his hand at her waist.

He placed his lips close to her ear. "Didn't mean to startle you. I'm so glad you're here. How long do you plan to stay?"

"We'll go back to Houston tomorrow, and I fly home on Sunday."

"Is it possible for you to spend the night at my place tonight? I'd get you back over here early."

She could feel her face glowing red. She turned and looked at him. "Wouldn't that be a little obvious?"

He sighed. "Yeah, I guess it would." He ran his hand along her spine and she shivered. "I planned to call you next week."

"Oh?" She picked up a plate, hoping he couldn't see how much her hands shook. She took a spoonful of each item, and her plate still was overflowing when she reached Jake. He placed ribs and sliced beef on her already-full plate.

"Hey, Jordan. Good to see you," Jake said. "Haven't seen much of you these days."

"I've been particularly busy for the past few weeks. Hopefully, things will slow down a little for me and we'll have some time to visit."

Janeen and Jordan stepped away, and Jordan led her to one of the picnic tables under a spreading live oak tree. Once she sat, Jordan asked, "What can I get you to drink?"

"Tea will be fine."

"Be right back."

She watched him move away. He had a loose-limbed way of walking that set off all her buttons, and he knew where each and every one of them were located.

He returned with two large glasses of iced tea and sat down across from her. "I'll always think of Jake's barbecues with pleasure since I met you at the one he had last month."

Janeen nodded but her attention was on the food, which was delicious. Jordan ate just as quietly. When they finished eating, he said, "Would you like to visit the black stallion? I'll bring you back here once you've seen him."

Was that anything like looking at his etchings? She grinned. "I'd like that," she said.

"Good. I'll let Jake know so he won't think we're skipping out on the celebration. We'll be back in plenty of time for the fireworks display."

She walked beside him. "I'll tell Lindsey."

They separated and Janeen went into the house. Lindsey was coming down the stairway. They both spoke at the same time.

"Oh, there you are!"

They looked at each other and laughed.

Janeen said, "Jordan's taking me over to see the black stallion that I befriended when I was here last month."

"Oh, how nice of him," Lindsey replied with a grin. "I am curious about one thing, though. Who's going to be the first to admit that you're in love with the other?"

"Dream on, my friend. It will never happen."

"Well, have fun," Lindsey said with a wave of her hand, and walked outside.

The problem with falling head over heels for someone was being so vulnerable to getting hurt. Who in the world said that falling in love is wonderful?

Once in the truck, Jordan reached for her hand. "There's no reason to be scrunched up against the door. I won't bite." He raised her fingers to his lips. "Nibble a little, but that's all," he added with a grin.

The first thing she noticed when they pulled into the ranch yard was the house. White paint made it sparkle and the black shutters at the windows made a nice contrast.

Jordan helped her out of the truck by picking her up at the waist and carefully setting her on the ground. Once again she got a brief scent of his aftershave that immediately reminded her of being in bed with him. She knew she was blushing.

She looked toward the pen where the stallion stayed and said, "Where is he?"

"I've turned him out into a larger pasture with a few horses. He's definitely interested in one of the mares."

He took her hand, and they walked through the barn to the back doors. The horse was peacefully grazing in a pasture with two mares.

They leaned on the fence. "Oh, he looks wonderful," Janeen said. "He's gained some weight since I was here, hasn't he?"

"Not surprising since he eats like a—" He shrugged.

She laughed. She realized that Jordan was as nervous as she was and that helped her relax a little.

Jordan whistled and the grazing horses looked up. The others went back to eating and the black stallion stared at them. His ears pricked forward. He started moving around the pasture, stepping high in a canter with his neck and tail held high.

"Would you look at that?" she whispered.

"He's definitely showing off now that you're here."

She looked at Jordan. "Do you think he recognizes me?"

"There's no doubt about that. He fell in love with you right away." He cleared his throat. "It took me a little longer."

Janeen looked at him, stunned by his remark. "Jordan?" she whispered.

He shrugged. "No sense in me pretending that I haven't fallen for you. You knew that when I showed up in New York."

She shook her head. "No. No, I didn't."

He lifted an eyebrow. "So you think I go to bed with every beautiful woman I meet?" He studied her for a moment. "I guess you do. Somehow I thought that you understood what that night meant for me. My mistake." He turned away. "Let's hunt up some carrots, shall we?"

Fifteen

Jordan's long strides quickly took him out of the barn and toward the house. Janeen had to hurry to catch up with him. He opened the back door leading into the kitchen and waited for her.

"Jordan, I—"

"You don't have to say anything. I needed to admit it to you. It's no big deal."

"But—" Janeen stopped speaking as she stepped into the kitchen. She couldn't believe the changes in the room. New cabinets, new appliances and new flooring greeted her.

Jordan stepped around her and went to the large, double-door refrigerator/freezer. He opened the door and reached into the vegetable drawer.

"When did you do this?" she managed to ask. "It's absolutely beautiful. The tile on the floor makes such a difference to the room."

He glanced around. "Just a project I decided to do. It isn't completed." He got a few carrots, closed the door to the fridge and handed them to her. "I've spoiled the stallion. I admit it. One carrot is no longer enough." He headed back outside.

Instead of following him out the door, Janeen peeked into the hallway. She spotted the changes in the living room through the arched doorway and walked into the room. He'd bought new furniture for the room. He'd set up an entertainment center that held his television and stereo equipment.

Janeen slowly turned in a circle in the middle of the room, noting lamps on new side tables and artwork on the walls. She saw Jordan leaning against the doorway, watching her. She'd thought he'd left.

"When did you find time to do all of this?"

"Oh, I squeezed out some extra time here and there. I take it you like it."

She hurried to him and threw her arms around his neck, hugging him. "You've done a wonderful job. You did all of this on your own?"

He wrapped his arms around her waist and pulled her against him. With a half smile, he replied, "I had some help." His lips were a couple inches away from hers.

Once again, Janeen found herself initiating an embrace with him. Flustered, she removed her arms from his neck, but before she could move, Jordan kissed her. It wasn't a tentative kiss. The kiss jumped several stages, quickly escalating to hot and passionate and causing her knees to buckle. He tightened his hold around her waist and continued to kiss her until they were both out of breath.

After taking a few deep breaths, Jordan said, "This isn't a good time to show you the changes I've made in the bedrooms." She could see that, despite his light tone, his eyes gave away the seriousness of his remark. He stepped away from her and took her hand. "Let's go feed the stallion," he said.

He was right. Of course he was right. Jumping into bed again at this point in their relationship—whatever it was— would be the worst possible thing to do. Her body vehemently argued with her reasonable acceptance. How could he kiss her like that and be able to walk away?

They returned to the pasture. The stallion spotted them and moved a little closer.

She held out a carrot. "I brought you something, you beautiful thing. Will you let me feed it to you?"

The stallion looked over at Jordan and rumbled in his chest.

"That was easy to interpret," Jordan said with a grin.

Janeen slipped the carrots under the fence and turned away. "Are you having any luck with getting him to accept you?"

"I've been working with him and he's coming along—very slowly—but at least he's no longer going crazy when I come into his pen."

"You've done a wonderful job with him."

"That's what they pay me for," he replied, obviously embarrassed and trying to cover.

"Oh, so someone bought him?"

He tugged on his ear. "Uh, no. I decided to keep him." He glanced at his watch. "I should get you back to Jake's place."

Janeen dutifully followed him out to the truck. He lifted her up into the cab of the truck. They were silent on the return trip. It wasn't until he was helping her out of the truck at Jake's that she spoke. She waited until her feet were on the ground before she said, "Just for the record—and not that it really matters—I happen to be in love with you, too."

She turned and went in search of Lindsey.

She was in love with him? Jordan stared at her as she walked away. Was that why— He stopped. Wow. That was the very last thing he expected to hear from her.

What did it mean? Would she marry him if he asked? Would she be willing to move to Texas?

The only way he would know the answers would be to ask her. Sounded easy enough. Of course finding the words to discuss his feelings—and hers—would be far from easy for him.

He looked for Janeen but she'd disappeared.

Jordan noted that several people had already left or were in the process of leaving. He spotted Jake cleaning up the cooking pots and utensils and walked over to him.

Jake glanced up with a smile and did a double take. "Did you get the license of the truck that must have run over you? You look like you're in shock."

"I'm okay," he muttered. He joined Jake in clearing the area. Jared wandered outside and saw them. "I was wondering what happened to you guys," he said, his hands stuck in his back jean pockets. He looked at Jake. "Once again you've thrown a successful barbecue, bro. Thanks for all the hard work."

"You know me. I enjoy it."

"I came out to tell you that we've decided to head back to Houston this afternoon instead of waiting until morning. I've been traveling and would dearly love to sleep in my own bed tonight," Jared said.

"Understandable," Jake replied.

"Excuse me, will you?" Jordan asked, and without waiting for an answer he headed inside the house. Once there, he looked around. The house appeared to be full of people, but he didn't see Janeen anywhere. He tried to remain polite as first one and then another friend or family member stopped him to say hello. He was rapidly running out of patience when he saw her coming down the stairs. He patted an uncle's back and said, "Hold that thought. I'll be back in a minute." He stopped Janeen in the hallway. "We need to talk."

Startled, she took a step back. "Now?" she asked faintly.

"Jared mentioned that you're going back today."

She nodded. "Yes."

He looked around at the people standing around visiting, took her arm and hurried her into Jake's office. As soon as they were inside, he closed and locked the door.

Her eyes widened.

He attempted to smile. "I'm not going to attack you, in case you're wondering."

"Okay," she said. She clasped her hands behind her.

Jordan took a deep breath, hoping he'd be able to find the right words to tell her how he felt. "I'm not good at this…and I have a lousy track record, I know." He paused and coughed, his throat bone dry. "I, uh, that is, if you *are* in love with me, I'd really like to talk about the possibility that you might want to—" He paused, searching for words. After taking a deep breath, his words finally rushed out. "—move to Texas and maybe, uh, you know—" he waved his hand "—marry me."

She stared at him as though he'd spoken another language. "Did you say marry you? Oh, Jordan, you don't have to say that just because I told you how I feel about you. I understand how you feel about marriage, I really do. You're just saying that because—"

"I'm saying it because I've been miserable without you. I'm saying it because despite our different lifestyles, I can't get you out of my mind. I'm saying it because I want you in my life. I don't know how we'll work things out regarding where we live. I'm willing to do whatever's necessary to keep you in my life."

He suddenly sat down in one of the chairs because he knew his knees weren't going to be able to hold him up much longer. He reached behind her back, took her hand and gently guided her to his lap. He draped his arms around her and nuzzled behind her ear. "I've never felt this way about another woman and, frankly, it's eating me alive. I want you in my life. Anyway I can have you. You may not love me enough to be uprooted from everything you know, and I can live with that rather than lose you. I'll spend as much time as I can in New York."

Thankfully she stopped him from blithering on in his current state of panic at the thought of her leaving today by cupping his face and kissing him.

Oh, this is what he'd needed, more than food or air. He

wrapped his arms around her and kissed her with a sense of desperation. He shook with emotion and it was a long time before they finally drew apart.

Janeen looked at him and traced his jaw with her finger. Finally, she said, "I think we can consider ourselves engaged then, don't you? We can work out the details as we go along."

He swallowed. Hard. "Then you'll marry me," he said slowly. This was not the time to misunderstand her.

"That's what engagements generally signify, yes."

"Okay, then. We'll get married." He waited a moment and then asked, "When?"

She blinked. "I really haven't gotten that far in my thinking. A proposal from you was the last thing I was expecting. I need to catch my breath." She remained silent, and he fought to hide his impatience. "You probably want a long engagement, so—"

"No! No long engagement. I'd marry you today if I could."

She laughed and gave him a quick kiss. "I don't believe that's possible. Besides, I need to tell my parents." She paused and studied him. "Could we compromise?"

Uh-oh, he knew there'd be a catch in there somewhere. "What sort of compromise?" he cautiously asked.

"I will move to Texas to live with you."

"Thank you," he said, kissing her at length. He thought about the locked door and how much he wanted her. Would it be possible to—

She leaned back in his arms. "The compromise will be—and I know this will be tough for you—is that we marry in Connecticut, which means a huge wedding that my mother's wanted to plan since I was born."

That announcement certainly wiped out any thought of making love to her. Her suggestion put the fear of God in him as though her mother had suddenly appeared in the room. He'd met her mother. He had a very good idea of the type of wedding she would want for Janeen. He briefly closed his eyes.

Janeen went on when he didn't say anything. "I swear she's been making lists as soon as I was born and she discovered I was a girl. Mom means well—she really does."

"I understand her love for her daughter, which gives us something important in common."

"It's just that I can't disappoint her now that I've finally found the man I want to spend the rest of my life with."

She caressed his cheek. "Do you love me enough to be part of such an extravaganza?"

He coughed. "Guess that would be a deal breaker if I wasn't, huh? We couldn't just go get married and then tell everybody?" he added hopefully.

Janeen looked as though she was trying to hide a smile. However, he couldn't see anything amusing about this conversation.

"I suppose we could," she slowly replied. "Of course my mother will never speak to either of us ever again…and then you have the fact that whatever makes Mom unhappy soon makes Dad unhappy because he has to listen to her carry on about it."

"Okay, okay. I get it. All right. We'll get married back East. Could you possibly move here next week while your mother is planning all this?"

That time, he saw her lips twitch. "You mean, you want me to move in with you before we're married?" she asked, pretending to be shocked. "What will the neighbors say!"

"I can see you're getting quite a lot of enjoyment out of this, aren't you?"

Before she could answer, someone rattled the door knob. He heard Lindsey say, "Janeen? Are you in here? Jared's ready to leave."

Janeen unwrapped her arms from around him, stood and hurried to the door. He stood and faced this first hurdle. They would have to tell everybody. Most of the time he enjoyed being a part of a large family…but not today.

Today, he had to face the fact that he had to announce to everyone that—once again—he was engaged. He might as well brace himself for all the teasing that would be coming his way.

Sixteen

Janeen waited until the children were in bed and Jared had gone upstairs for his shower before she told Lindsey what had transpired between Jordan and her. Lindsey grabbed her by the shoulders, let out a modified whoop and said, "Oh, Janeen, that's wonderful! He proposed! You never expected to hear that from him." She paused and looked closely at Janeen. "You don't seem too thrilled, though. Is it because of how far away you are from him?"

"I'm very thrilled. I mean, I'm still wondering if I dreamed the whole thing!"

Lindsey stepped back from her and folded her arms. With a stern look she asked, "But?"

Janeen had thought telling Lindsey would be easier than it was. She was presently suffering from a bad case of dry mouth. "Do you have any sodas here?"

"Yes. In the fridge. Are you trying to change the subject, because if you are, don't even think about it."

"No, I'm just a little dry." She went into the kitchen and called back, "Do you want anything?"

"No, thanks."

Janeen opened her drink, poured it into a glass and took a long swallow before returning to the living room. She sank down onto the sofa with a sigh. After another long drink, she looked at Lindsey and said, "Have you given any thought to how my mother is going to react when she finds out I'm getting married and moving halfway across the country?"

"Oh." Then Lindsey grinned. "So you *are* going to move here!" She threw her arms around Janeen. "Do you realize how much I've wanted us to be closer in order to have more visits?"

"Well, your wish is about to be granted. Only, how do I deal with Mom?"

"Yeah."

They sat in silence for several minutes. Janeen finished her drink and stared off into space. There were times when she wished she didn't have such a vivid imagination.

"You're not going to let her talk you out of marrying him, though, right?" Lindsey finally asked.

"Absolutely not! The thing is that he suggested we get married like—oh—today was his suggestion."

Lindsey laughed. "I like his style."

"At least he didn't suggest he drag me by my hair back to his cave."

"Oh, come on. He isn't that bad."

Janeen sighed. "Why did I have to go and fall for a rancher? In Texas?"

"It could be worse. He might have lived in Montana—or Idaho."

"I've never visited there," Janeen replied morosely.

"Ah, I get it," Lindsey said. "So now it's my fault that you came to Texas and fell in love."

"No, of course not. I really do love him. Oh, Lindsey. If you could have seen him. I've never seen anyone quite so nervous before. It must have been really tough for him to admit he was willing to get married."

"And to a Yankee, at that!" They drifted into silence once again. Finally, Lindsey said, "You can do it. I have faith in you. After all, you've had to deal with your mother all your life."

"True. And during all that time, I've heard her talk about how much she was looking forward to planning my wedding. At least Jordan agreed to get married back East. That's a big concession for him, you know." She thought about her conversation with Jordan. "You know what I think? I think he thinks that I'll change my mind once I get back home."

"Should he be worried?"

Janeen shook her head. "Of course not. I told him I'd marry him and that I would move to Texas to be with him. Nothing will stand in my way…including my mother!"

Lindsey's smile was radiant. "That a girl. That wasn't so difficult to face, was it? Did you decide on a date?"

"Are you kidding? Mother will expect at least a year's notice to prepare for the event."

"Did you tell him that?"

"Absolutely not. It was hard enough to tell him that I'd like to get married there."

"Has he any idea what your mother is going to make of this opportunity?"

"Not really. I did warn him about that, but he's never seen Mom in action."

"He must really be in love with you."

Janeen smiled. "I know. Oh! I forgot to tell you that Jordan has remodeled his house. I think he did it for me. It's really nice inside. He showed me everything but the bedrooms. I guess he didn't trust himself, or maybe he didn't trust me not to take advantage of him!"

Their eyes met and they both broke into hilarious laughter.

"What are you guys drinking?" Jared said, yawning as he came down the stairs.

"I'm so sorry, Jared," Janeen said, embarrassed. "We must have woken you up."

He was dressed in a bathrobe. He leaned over Lindsey's chair and kissed her cheek. "Nope. I haven't been to sleep. I'm lonesome up there all by myself." He glanced at Janeen and winked.

The women stood. Lindsey turned to Jared and said, "Jordan asked Janeen to marry him before we left. They were in Jake's office, which was why we had trouble finding them."

Jared stared first at one and then the other. "Are you serious?"

Janeen nodded. "I'm serious and so was he."

"What did you tell him?"

Janeen grinned. "That I would."

"Hey, that's great. Welcome to the family." He hugged her. "You've also made Lindsey very happy. You'll be within driving distance from each other." He grinned and asked, "So when's the big day?"

Jared stared at the two women in dismay when they looked at each other and laughed like a pair of hyenas. Lindsey took his hand and said, "With that, I agree that it's time to go to bed." She kissed his chin. "It will all work out, I'm sure."

Janeen watched them go upstairs. She heard Jared say in a soft voice, "What did I say?" before they disappeared.

She wished that she and Jordan were already married and the planning was well behind them.

As soon as Janeen returned home Sunday, she called her mother. "Once again I'm back home."

"Why, hello, darling. Did you have a good time?"

"Very." She paused. "I was thinking about coming up for the weekend if that's okay with you."

"Of course. You know that we enjoy having you here."

"Good. I'll see you then."

Janeen hung up and looked around her apartment. She'd lived here for several years. It was convenient and affordable and she had felt like dancing with glee when she had found it.

She would be busy this week, clearing out the place, throwing stuff away, finding someone who might want her furniture. She groaned. Then she thought of Jordan and knew that all the work she needed to do was going to be worth it.

Everything she'd heard about him had been true. He wasn't as comfortable around people as he was with his animals. He seemed especially uneasy around women. However, the man was dynamite when she got him turned on, and it didn't seem to take much to do that. She smiled. Somehow she would get him used to having her around, even if she had to keep him in bed most of the time to help him adjust to her presence!

Later, as she was getting ready for bed, her phone rang. When she picked up, she discovered Jordan was on the line. "How was your flight?"

Just the sound of his voice made her knees go weak. "Uneventful, my favorite kind."

"I need to ask you something. Were you really at Jake's place for the Fourth?"

Was he kidding? Did he secretly have a drinking problem? "I do believe I was. Why?"

She heard a big sigh of relief. "Good. I was afraid I'd dreamed the whole thing," he said.

"Having nightmares about asking me to marry you?"

"Nothing like that. I was afraid I'd dreamed the part where you said yes."

She laughed and he soon joined her. "Nope. Guess you're stuck with me."

"That's why I called."

Her heart stuttered as if it was ready to stop. After a moment, she said, "Okay."

"I was thinking that we could get married between Christmas and New Year's. I'd like to get stuck with you as soon as possible. What do you think?"

Her heart picked up its rhythm. "I could have sworn you preferred long engagements," she said, picking her words carefully.

"Not anymore. I'm a firm believer in getting you into my bed as soon as possible."

"I think I've managed to solve that problem."

He laughed. "Great. How?"

"I'm moving to Texas as soon as I get packed. I'll probably be ready this time next month."

"In that case, I'll be up there to help you."

"That was my good news."

Silence greeted her. Finally, he asked, "What is the bad news?"

"I'm going to spend the weekend with my parents so I can tell them we're getting married. My mother may find December a little soon to get prepared."

"Well, when do you think she'd like to have it?"

"Sometime in a year to eighteen months."

"What! That's ridiculous."

"That's why I'm not looking forward to this weekend. I'll need to stand strong on that point."

"You might want to point out to her that since she's not the one getting married, we would like a vote on this."

She laughed. "Oh, Jordan. I love you so much!"

"Why don't you tell her that if she doesn't want to plan a wedding by then, we can go to Vegas. Unless you really want the big, formal wedding, too," he cautiously added.

She laughed. "Not in the least. I'd prefer a nice, quiet wedding."

"Then tell her that."

After a long pause, she drawled, "Okay."

"I haven't been able to sleep since you left. The men working with me are complaining that I've turned into a grizzly bear."

"Uh-huh. I believe I met that grizzly a few weeks ago."

He chuckled. "And yet…knowing the worst about me… you're still ready to marry me."

"Maybe I'm just a glutton for punishment."

Neither of them spoke for a while. Finally, Jordan said in a low voice, "I wish you were here."

"So do I. That's why I'm coming down there as soon as I can.

I have to give notice at the museum and deal with the lease on my apartment, but it's worth all of that to know I'll be with you."

They hung up and Janeen stared at the phone for a long time. She loved Jordan so much.

"You're doing what!?" her mother said.

Janeen sat across the table from her parents Saturday morning. She'd gotten in late the night before and gone directly to bed. She'd seen them for the first time over coffee this morning.

Janeen glanced at her father, who admittedly looked surprised. "I didn't know you've been seeing anyone," he finally said.

"You can't be serious!" her mother continued.

Their breakfasts arrived. Janeen looked up at Grace, their cook, and said, "Looks scrumptious." Grace smiled, gave her a quick wink and, after placing their plates in front of them, left the room.

Janeen began to eat.

Her mother watched her for a moment and finally asked, "Is that all you're going to tell us? That you're getting married? Could we at least know who you plan to marry?"

Janeen sipped her coffee. "Absolutely. I'm going to marry Jordan Crenshaw and move to Texas."

Her mother turned parchment white. Her dad nodded and said, "He seems to be a likable person. I didn't know you were still in touch with him."

Janeen grinned. "He doesn't communicate all that much but when he does he can clearly make his wishes known."

Her mother took a drink of water, her other hand resting on her chest. "You could have given us some warning."

"Sorry. It just happened. I thought I should tell you in person, rather than by phone. We just got engaged on the Fourth of July."

Her mother looked at Janeen's hand. "No ring?" she asked with a raised brow.

Janeen smiled. "Not yet."

"Well. If this is what you want, I'll get busy making arrangements. Have you decided when you want to marry?"

"Between Christmas and New Year's."

"Noooo!" Her mother shook her head in horror. "I can't possibly—"

"Mom. Listen to me. I love you very much. I know you've always wanted me to have an elaborate wedding, but that's not what I want. So if you want to plan something by, say, December 28, he's agreed that we can have the wedding here." She looked at her dad. "Meanwhile, I'm moving to Texas in a few weeks."

The silence in the room grew until it became deafening. Janeen continued to eat.

Her dad finally spoke. "You know, Susan, this really isn't about us. I know she's our only child but what we want for her is her happiness." He looked at Janeen. "I hope Jordan realizes how lucky he is to win your love."

That did it. Janeen began to cry.

Seventeen

As soon as Janeen walked past security at the airport, she spotted Jordan in the crowd of people waiting for passengers to disembark. As it turned out, he'd been unable to come to New York to help with the move and she hadn't seen him in weeks.

He seemed to see her at the same time because he smiled and started toward her. As soon as he reached her, he picked her off her feet and kissed her until she knew she was turning several shades of red.

When he finally let her down, he took her hand. "Let's get your luggage and get out of here."

"I just have two bags. I shipped everything else."

He chuckled. "My kind of woman."

Once they reached his truck, he looked at his watch. "It's almost ten o'clock."

"I know. I'm sorry the plane was delayed. Thunderstorms."

He started the truck and backed out of the parking space. "I thought we'd stay here in Austin overnight and head back to the ranch in the morning."

She looked at him. "When did you happen to decide that?"

"Oh…about noon when I knew that whenever you got here we weren't going far."

Yes. He was a man of few words, and what he did say was straight and to the point.

He pulled into the hotel's entrance and drove to the back. "I've already checked in," he said, parking the truck.

Once inside the hotel, he took her hand and they walked to the room. He opened the door with a key card and stepped back for her to go inside.

The lamps were on when she walked in and there seemed to be flowers everywhere—on the table, on the dresser and on the bedside table. She looked at him in surprise.

He smiled and said, "Welcome to Texas." He held out his hand, and when she took it, he slipped a diamond ring on the third finger of her left hand. The large stone was surrounded by smaller diamonds, causing the ring to glitter in the soft light.

"Oh, Jordan," she whispered. "It's beautiful."

"I'm glad you like it. So now it's official, I guess." The look in his eyes left no doubt about what he wanted.

"I guess it is," she replied and started unbuttoning his shirt. That was the only encouragement he needed.

He gathered her in his arms and sat on the side of the bed. She shoved the shirt off his shoulders. When she reached for his belt, he stopped her. "I've waited too long and I don't want to end this too soon."

Somehow they stripped off their clothes and were in bed. His urgency was evident, but Janeen didn't mind in the least.

He caressed her body with his hands, his mouth and his tongue, until she was begging for him to end the torment. He ignored her until she thought she was going to lose her mind. Only then did he ease inside her, causing her release to rocket through her. He set a rapid pace, and she tightened around him once again. When he climaxed, she was right there with him.

He rolled to his side and began to caress her again. He cupped her breasts and teased them with his tongue. She felt his erection against her side.

"I may never get enough of you," he replied and spent most of the night proving it to her.

Many hours later Janeen stirred and stretched, suddenly feeling sore muscles. She turned her head and saw that Jordan was already up and dressed. He sat in a chair pulled up to the bed, watching her.

Embarrassed, she felt around for the sheet.

"Honey, you're a little late if you want to be modest around me."

She sat up and pushed her hair out of her face. "How long have you been up?" He grinned at her, obviously amused. "Okay, when did you wake up?"

"The usual time."

"But you couldn't have gotten much sleep."

"Enough."

She finally found the sheet and wrapped it around her when she got up. "I'll go shower," she mumbled and with as much dignity as possible—considering the situation—went into the bathroom.

Once they were at the ranch, Jordan said, "I was so busy welcoming you to Texas that I forgot all about asking how your visit with your parents went."

"Very well. As usual Dad stepped in and helped me convince Mom that since this is my wedding, we should be able to decide certain things without her help." She smiled. "We're getting married on December 28."

"Thank God. Is it going to be a huge wedding?"

"Depends on how much she can do between now and then. Knowing Mom, she'll pull it off. She's very determined, you know."

"Somehow that doesn't surprise me."

"I suppose Jack will stand up for you."

"Who else? He'd kill me if I chose someone else. He'll probably break out in hives from being around all the trappings of a large wedding. Who are you going to have?"

When she answered, he said it with her. "Lindsey."

"So what do we have to do to get ready for this momentous occasion?"

"For me, nothing. Mom's having my dress made. She took all my measurements before I left. As for you, invite everyone you want who's willing to travel back East during the holidays."

He groaned. "That will be the entire Crenshaw clan. Won't your mother be surprised?"

She laughed. "I can hardly wait to see her face. As long as you're there, that's all that matters to me." She looked around. "Which reminds me...I haven't seen the bedroom. Would you care to show it to me?"

"I'm certain that something can be arranged."

Epilogue

Spring in Texas would always be Janeen's favorite time of year. Wherever she looked, wild flowers grew in multicolored splendor. She'd had no idea bluebonnets were so beautiful.

She sat on the porch in the padded rocking chair that Jordan had bought for her. He was such a sweetheart. He'd hired two new hands so he could spend a little more time with her. He'd told her his business had grown so much that he'd have no trouble paying the extra men.

She leaned her head back on the chair and closed her eyes. The next thing she knew, the screen door opened and her mother came out, carrying a tray with iced tea and snacks.

Janeen smiled. "Looks great, Mom. Thanks."

Susan returned the smile and set the tray on the table between their chairs. "How are you feeling?"

"A little better."

"That's good. You had me a little worried. I would have thought any morning sickness would be over by now."

"Believe me, so did I."

The two women looked out over the ranch. Finally, Janeen said, "Dad seems to be enjoying being here on the ranch, doesn't he?"

Susan nodded. "Your father is quite impressed with Jordan's skill with horses. He said his breeding program is one of the best he's ever seen."

"It's nice to see him so enthusiastic."

Silence fell between them once again.

Eventually, Susan said, "Was the doctor certain you're carrying twins? There have never been twins in our family."

"Oh, but there are Crenshaw twins. Remember Jordan's identical brother at the wedding?"

"How can I forget? I was so embarrassed when I kept calling him Jordan."

"I'm sure he's used to it. And, yes, I'm definitely having twins. I saw the sonogram."

Susan sighed. "Having one at a time is difficult enough. I worry about you having to go through such an ordeal."

"Oh, it will be worth it once they're here."

Susan took a sip of her tea. "Oh, there they are," she said, nodding toward the barn.

Janeen grinned when she saw her knight in shining armor and her father come out of the barn and walk toward them.

Susan immediately went inside for more glasses.

Once he reached the porch, Jordan leaned on her chair, tilting her forward, and kissed her. "You okay, sweetheart?"

She nodded. "The doctor assures me I'll be over this phase in another week or two."

Jordan straightened and sat nearby.

Janeen looked at her dad. "What do you have planned for the rest of the day?"

He settled into her mother's chair. "Your mom wants to go shopping in Austin or San Antonio. She'll probably buy out the baby departments in most of the stores. You're welcome to go with us."

Janeen smiled. "Thanks, but I tend to get carsick these days."

Her dad settled back into the chair. "You know, Texas really has a lot going for it. So much open space and beautiful countryside. I wouldn't mind moving here once I retire."

Janeen leaned toward him and whispered, "Don't let Mom hear you say that. She'll go into cardiac arrest!"

He patted her hand. "Don't worry. Once those grandbabies arrive, she'll be all for the idea."

Her mother returned. "Here you go," she said, handing each of the men a full glass of iced tea.

Her dad said, "I think today is perfect for shopping. Where would you like to start?"

Susan shrugged. "Doesn't matter." She smiled at Janeen. "With Jordan here, I know you'll manage just fine without us."

Janeen winked at Jordan. "Well, I'll do my best."

Her father asked, "I've been meaning to ask you, do you want your mom and I here when the babies come?"

"Of course, Dad. I couldn't do it without you."

Her dad chuckled. "Oh, I figured you could handle it, but we'd like to be there when they arrive." He put his arm around Susan, and they smiled at each other.

Jordan waited until her parents left before he asked, "Would you like to visit Beauty?"

When she'd first moved to Texas, Jordan suggested that Janeen name the stallion.

"His name is Beauty," she had said.

"Beauty? That's not a name for a stallion."

"He won't care. He's secure in his masculinity."

"I'd love to see Beauty. It's been a few days since I last saw him."

Jordan took her hand and helped her out of the chair. She placed her hand on her protruding stomach. "I can't imagine how I'll get around when it's closer to my time. I already feel like a cow."

Jordan stepped back and studied her. Finally, he shook his head. "You don't look like a cow."

"Thank you for that." They walked toward the pasture.

"No, I think I'd describe you as looking more like a beached whale—a baby whale, of course," he added with a grin.

She punched his shoulder, laughing.

As soon as they arrived at the fence, Jordan whistled. The stallion was in a large pasture with a few other horses. His head jerked up at the sound. The others glanced up before continuing to nibble on the grass, and he started trotting toward them.

Janeen had learned never to leave the house without carrots and apples.

The horse didn't hesitate as he approached them. He stopped at the fence and leaned his head toward her. "You really are spoiled, you know," Janeen said softly, running her hand along his neck. She handed him an apple. He gently lipped the fruit into his mouth, being careful not to bite her, before he chomped down.

"I'm so glad you kept him," she said, leaning against Jordan. "He's such a sweetheart."

"I knew as soon as I saw you making up to him last summer that he wasn't leaving here. He tolerates me now, but he'll always be your horse." He leaned down and kissed the tip of her nose.

Jordan adjusted his steps to hers as they returned to the house. "I feel guilty every time I look at you."

Janeen looked up in surprise. "What on earth for?"

"If I weren't so desperately in love with you, we might have held off having babies for a while," he said, patting her tummy. "I still can't seem to leave you alone."

"I wouldn't want it any other way, darlin'," she said with a drawl. "I'm doing everything I can to help the cause. Otherwise, Texas might run out of Crenshaws!"

He laughed and pulled her close to his side. "That will never happen!"

Janeen was inclined to agree with him.

* * * * *

*Celebrate 60 years of pure reading pleasure
with Harlequin® Books!*

*Harlequin Romance® is celebrating by showering you with
DIAMOND BRIDES in February 2009.
Six stories that promise to bring a touch of sparkle to your
life, with diamond proposals and dazzling weddings,
sparkling brides and gorgeous grooms!*

*Enjoy a sneak peek at Caroline Anderson's
TWO LITTLE MIRACLES,
available February 2009 from Harlequin Romance®.*

"I'VE FOUND HER."

Max froze.

It was what he'd been waiting for since June, but now—now he was almost afraid to voice the question. His heart stalling, he leaned slowly back in his chair and scoured the investigator's face for clues. "Where?" he asked, and his voice sounded rough and unused, like a rusty hinge.

"In Suffolk. She's living in a cottage."

Living. His heart crashed back to life, and he sucked in a long, slow breath. All these months he'd feared—

"Is she well?"

"Yes, she's well."

He had to force himself to ask the next question. "Alone?"

The man paused. "No. The cottage belongs to a man called John Blake. He's working away at the moment, but he comes and goes."

God. He felt sick. So sick he hardly registered the next few words, but then gradually they sank in. "She's got *what?*"

"Babies. Twin girls. They're eight months old."

"Eight—" he echoed under his breath. "They must be his."

He was thinking out loud, but the P.I. heard and corrected him.

"Apparently not. I gather they're hers. She's been there since mid-January last year, and they were born during the summer— June, the woman in the post office thought. She was more than helpful. I think there's been a certain amount of speculation about their relationship."

He'd just bet there had. God, he was going to kill her. Or Blake. Maybe both of them.

"Of course, looking at the dates, she was presumably pregnant when she left you, so they could be yours, or she could have been having an affair with this Blake character before..."

He glared at the unfortunate P.I. "Just stick to your job. I can do the math," he snapped, swallowing the unpalatable possibility that she'd been unfaithful to him before she'd left. "Where is she? I want the address."

"It's all in here," the man said, sliding a large envelope across the desk to him. "With my invoice."

"I'll get it seen to. Thank you."

"If there's anything else you need, Mr. Gallagher, any further information—"

"I'll be in touch."

"The woman in the post office told me Blake was away at the moment, if that helps," he added quietly, and opened the door.

Max stared down at the envelope, hardly daring to open it, but when the door clicked softly shut behind the P.I., he eased up the flap, tipped it and felt his breath jam in his throat as the photos spilled out over the desk.

Oh, Lord, she looked gorgeous. Different, though. It took him a moment to recognize her, because she'd grown her hair, and it was tied back in a ponytail, making her look younger and somehow freer. The blond highlights were gone, and it was back to its natural soft golden-brown, with a little curl in the end of the ponytail that he wanted to thread his finger through and tug, just gently, to draw her back to him.

Crazy. She'd put on a little weight, but it suited her. She looked well and happy and beautiful, but oddly, considering how desperate he'd been for news of her for the past year—one year, three weeks and two days, to be exact—it wasn't only Julia who held his attention after the initial shock. It was the babies sitting side by side in a supermarket trolley. Two identical and absolutely beautiful little girls.

* * * * *

When Max Gallagher hires a P.I. to find his estranged wife, Julia, he discovers she's not alone—she has twin baby girls, and they might be his. Now workaholic Max has just two weeks to prove that he can be a wonderful husband and father to the family he wants to treasure.

Look for TWO LITTLE MIRACLES by Caroline Anderson, available February 2009 from Harlequin Romance®.

CELEBRATE
60 YEARS
OF PURE READING PLEASURE
WITH **HARLEQUIN**®!

We'll be spotlighting a different series
every month throughout 2009
to celebrate our 60th anniversary.

Look for Harlequin® Romance in February!

**Harlequin® Romance is celebrating by showering
you with Diamond Brides in February 2009.**

Six stories that promise to bring a touch of sparkle to
your life, with diamond proposals and dazzling weddings,
sparkling brides and gorgeous grooms!

Collect all six books in February 2009,
featuring *Two Little Miracles* by Caroline Anderson.

*Look for the Diamond Brides miniseries
in February 2009!*

www.eHarlequin.com   HRBRIDES09

HARLEQUIN® Romance®

This February the Harlequin® Romance series
will feature six Diamond Brides stories featuring
diamond proposals and gorgeous grooms.

Share your dream wedding proposal and you could WIN!

The most romantic entry will win a diamond
necklace and will inspire a proposal in one of
our upcoming Diamond Grooms books in 2010.

In 100 words or less, tell us the most romantic
way that you dream of being proposed to.

For more information, and to enter
the Diamond Brides Proposal contest, please visit
www.DiamondBridesProposal.com

Or mail your entry to us at:
IN THE U.S.: 3010 Walden Ave., P.O. Box 9069, Buffalo, NY 14269-9069
IN CANADA: 225 Duncan Mill Road, Don Mills, ON M3B 3K9

REQUEST YOUR FREE BOOKS!

2 FREE NOVELS PLUS 2 FREE GIFTS!

Silhouette® *Desire*®

Passionate, Powerful, Provocative!

YES! Please send me 2 FREE Silhouette Desire® novels and my 2 FREE gifts (gifts are worth about $10). After receiving them, if I don't wish to receive any more books, I can return the shipping statement marked "cancel". If I don't cancel, I will receive 6 brand-new novels every month and be billed just $4.05 per book in the U.S. or $4.74 per book in Canada, plus 25¢ shipping and handling per book and applicable taxes, if any*. That's a savings of almost 15% off the cover price! I understand that accepting the 2 free books and gifts places me under no obligation to buy anything. I can always return a shipment and cancel at any time. Even if I never buy another book, the two free books and gifts are mine to keep forever.

225 SDN ERVX 326 SDN ERVM

Name	(PLEASE PRINT)	
Address		Apt. #
City	State/Prov.	Zip/Postal Code

Signature (if under 18, a parent or guardian must sign)

Mail to the Silhouette Reader Service:
IN U.S.A.: P.O. Box 1867, Buffalo, NY 14240-1867
IN CANADA: P.O. Box 609, Fort Erie, Ontario L2A 5X3

Not valid to current subscribers of Silhouette Desire books.

Want to try two free books from another line?
Call 1-800-873-8635 or visit www.morefreebooks.com.

* Terms and prices subject to change without notice. N.Y. residents add applicable sales tax. Canadian residents will be charged applicable provincial taxes and GST. Offer not valid in Quebec. This offer is limited to one order per household. All orders subject to approval. Credit or debit balances in a customer's account(s) may be offset by any other outstanding balance owed by or to the customer. Please allow 4 to 6 weeks for delivery. Offer available while quantities last.

Your Privacy: Silhouette Books is committed to protecting your privacy. Our Privacy Policy is available online at www.eHarlequin.com or upon request from the Reader Service. From time to time we make our lists of customers available to reputable third parties who have a product or service of interest to you. If you would prefer we not share your name and address, please check here. ☐

SDES08R

You're invited to join our Tell Harlequin Reader Panel!

By joining our new reader panel you will:

- Receive Harlequin® books—they are FREE and yours to keep with no obligation to purchase anything!
- Participate in fun online surveys
- Exchange opinions and ideas with women just like you
- Have a say in our new book ideas and help us publish the best in women's fiction

In addition, you will have a chance to win great prizes and receive special gifts!
See Web site for details. Some conditions apply.
Space is limited.

To join, visit us at

www.TellHarlequin.com.

Tell
HARLEQUIN

COMING NEXT MONTH

#1921 MR. STRICTLY BUSINESS—Day Leclaire
Man of the Month
He'd always taken what he wanted, when he wanted it—but she wouldn't bend to those rules. Now she needs his help. His price? Her—back in his bed.

#1922 TEMPTED INTO THE TYCOON'S TRAP—
Emily McKay
The Hudsons of Beverly Hills
When he finds out that her secret baby is really his, he demands that she marry him. But their passion hasn't fizzled, and soon their marriage of convenience becomes very real.

#1923 CONVENIENT MARRIAGE, INCONVENIENT
HUSBAND—Yvonne Lindsay
Rogue Diamonds
She'd left him at the altar eight years ago, but now she needs him in order to gain her inheritance. Could this be his chance to teach her that one can't measure love with money?

#1924 RESERVED FOR THE TYCOON—Charlene Sands
Suite Secrets
His new events planner is trying to sabotage his hotel, but his attraction to her is like nothing he's ever felt. Will he choose to destroy her...or seduce her?

#1925 MILLIONAIRE'S SECRET SEDUCTION—
Jennifer Lewis
The Hardcastle Progeny
On discovering a beautiful woman's intentions to sue his father's company, he makes her a deal—her body in exchange for his silence.

#1926 THE C.O.O. MUST MARRY—Maxine Sullivan
Their fathers forced them to marry each other to save their families' fortunes. Will a former young love blossom again, or will secrets drive them apart?

SDCNMBPA0109